Eurydice's Lament

FROM THE SAME AUTHOR

Eurydice's Lament

by

Brian Stableford

A Black Coat Press Book

For Catherine.
B.S.

Visit our website at www.blackcoatpress.com

INTRODUCTORY NOTE

This novel is a sequel to the two short stories and the short novel contained in the Black Coat Press collection *The Wayward Muse*, in which many of the characters featured herein were introduced and one or two mentioned in passing here—most notably the morpheomorphist Eirene Magdelana—unfortunately perished. There is, however, no need to have read the previous volume to find this one perfectly comprehensible.

The stories are set on Mnemosyne, an island off the northern coast of what in our world is called France, although it never acquired that name in the alternative history of the story because it was not successfully invaded by the Franks, the Roman Empire having remained powerful and well-organized after the glorious career of its first great emperor, Julius Caesar, able to withstand or absorb all barbarian encroachments. The present novel reveals something of the difference that alteration in history made to the history of various religions and cults, albeit obliquely. Classical mythology, of course, remains identical in our world and the fictitious one.

B.S.

I. Black Snow

Perhaps it was foolish to set forth to walk all the way to the harbor when the sky was so full of low cloud, all the more so as the cold north-westerly wind that had been blowing that morning had dropped, leaving a dead calm suspended ponderously over the island. Any of the local fishermen, consulted for his expert prognosis, would have shaken his head sadly and advised me to stay indoors if I didn't want to end up soaked to the skin, or, at the very least, to order Jean-Jacques to harness the sociable and provide me with a modest shelter from the anticipated deluge.

I knew all that, but I set off anyway. The painting had not been going well, and I felt that I had been stranded in the Underworld all morning, in the midst of the clustering shades avid to hear the music that my Orpheus was playing—so avid that the actual silence surrounding me had come to seem oppressive and, by some strange effect of kinesthesia, suffocating. I felt that I needed air, light and an interval of meditation, such that a carriage cannot provide, even when Mnemosyne's roads are in a better conditions than they tend to be on a dull afternoon in October.

I had not even put on heavy boots, although I had exchanged the slippers I had been wearing in my studio for polished shoes, as if I were heading for some kind of organized social event, where I might met potential clients. One can never show too much polish to potential clients, from the glittering wit of the head to the shine of shoes that seem to be crying out to dance. Not that I do dance, of course; it would not fit in with the dignity of my current image. But one ought to seem able and prepared even for what dignity forbids, if one wants to maintain the kind of image that befits a true artist.

In a way, I was going to an organized social event: a reception of sorts. It would be a very select gathering, and the person for whom it was being held had no idea that any kind of reception would be waiting for him, but still, it was intended as a welcome, hastily arranged, in a slightly oblique fashion by no means typical of her, by Myrica Mavor, my agent. She was also the agent of the expected new arrival, who was coming all the way from the capital's Martyr's Mount in order to be my closest neighbor—and, Myrica doubtless hoped, my most piquant rival.

Myrica was a great belier in the stimulus of rivalry. Exactly what involvement she had had in the purchase of the late Monsieur de Toustain's house on behalf of her client I did not know, but I was sure that she was mixed up in it. Perhaps she had been trying to persuade Charles Parenot to relocate to the island for years—it would not be the first time she had urged one of her clients to do that—and had finally found the means to wear him down by promising him proximity to the greatest artist in the province.

On the other hand, I thought, *perhaps not*. If the allure of joining a select community dedicated to the highest principles of esthetics, at whose mysterious hub Myrica's patter had doubtless placed me, had not been sufficient bait, the mere fact of acquiring accommodation within a stone's throw of my personal factory of genius was unlikely to have tipped the balance.

Nor can the stone's throw be taken literally, I noted, as I passed by what been Toustain's house along the road that formed the promontory's spine, and glanced backwards at my own. *Even with the aid of a sling, a man without sin would not be able to cast a stone that far. A giant with a Medieval longbow might have been able to land an arrow on the roof, but even with a modern rifle...*

I cut off that thought. I was beginning to think like Myrica, in terms of enmity and rivalry. I did not want to do that. The idea of having another painter within sight of the dining-room window was not entirely appealing, but there was no reason at all why Charles Parenot should not be the most amicable of neighbors, and even a friend.

The Toustain house, as I continued to think of it— there would doubtless be time enough to adapt to the idea of "the Parenot house"—was dingy at present, having not been well-maintained externally. Whether it had been well-maintained internally I had no idea, never having crossed the threshold, but I suspected not. Unusually, for a man of his apparent quality, Toustain had only ever had one servant, an old crone who had died six months before him, and whose appearance had been so rebarbative that no one could possible suspect that he had not long survived her because he was grief-stricken at the loss of a secret mistress. More likely he had poisoned himself with his own cooking.

Normally, in spite of or because of the fact that I went past the Toustain house every time I went into town or returned therefrom, I never spared it any kind of glance, let alone the appraising inspection of a professional eye, but this time, I turned my head to study it in a quasi-clinical fashion, searching for an accurate adjective with which to sum it up.

Gloomy, I thought, *and not merely because the sky is so low and leaden, or because I know that a man was*

9

carried out of it in a coffin not long ago—a coffin that not a single mourner followed to the cemetery, or even the traditional stray dog.

I did not feel the slightest twinge of conscience. There had been no reason for me to step into that void, just because Toustain had left me a small and tokenistic legacy, of no considerable value, commercially or esthetically.

In any case, I thought, *a gloomy appearance in by no means suited to it. Monsieur de Toustain always seemed a dark and gloomy man, and even when the windows of his house were illuminated by vacillating candlelight, the edifice retained his personality, and never radiated any conspicuous warmth.*

The house was separated by more than two hundred long paces of bare heathland—no trees grew on the promontory, probably because the salt of the spindrift made its soil inhospitable to everything but coarse grass and heather—but there was no habitation nearer to mine. Once, there had been two fisherman's cots in a sheltered declivity at the extremity of the headland, where a small inlet permitted boats to be safely beached, but they had been abandoned long ago—more years than I cared to count. It was not that the fish were no longer there to be caught, but the economy of the island had shifted away from an attempted self-sufficiency that had never been better than marginal to the much more profitable business of servicing the summer visitors with whom it had become inexplicably fashionable. The artists' colony, whose establishment on the continental fringe was understandable, in terms of psychic geography, had been here long before then, but it was not until the aristocrats began to spend "vacations" here—vacations from what, I sometimes wondered, since, by definition, they did not work—that service industries had really begun to thrive.

Thus, the reclusive Monsieur de Toustain had been my nearest neighbor throughout the sixteen years since he had arrived on the island, and during that time he had been the perfect neighbor for an artist like me—which is to say that he had kept entirely to himself. If our paths had happened to intersect, as they inevitably did on occasion, since I had to walk past his house in order to go into town, we had greeted one another with scrupulous politeness, and even exchanged a few conventional remarks on the weather, but he was as taciturn as he was polite, and there was never a cross word between us, or any serious attempt at meaningful communication.

Apparently, he appreciated that near silence as much as I did. Otherwise, why would he have inserted a clause into his will bequeathing his books to me? Not that he had a large or precious collection, but some of the books had interesting engravings—that was presumably the reason that he had thought of leaving them to a painter—but it was still a gesture of kindness, from a man not habituated to such gestures, for which I really ought to feel a modicum of gratitude.

According to his notary, Maître Guillot, who had given me the good news with a strangely unctuous glee, and had supervised the transfer of the three crates of books from one house to the other with undue ceremony, it was the only individual bequest Toustain had made. All his other worldly goods had been left to the Island Council, to be sold for the benefit of the poor and needy. The books would not have made much difference to the benefit the poor and needy received—if they received anything at all once the members of the Council had dipped their sticky fingers into whatever sum remained after the auctioneer had taken his own cut—so I saw no need to feel guilt about having kept the books, even though they were still in the crates in which they had been delivered, because I had not yet been able to face the Herculean task of rearranging my cluttered shelves with sufficient ingenuity to make room for them.

It was not long after I had turned left on to the corniche that the snow began to fall. At first I was astonished that it was snow and not rain. Although some ancient fisherman or old Nicodemus Rham might have been able to contradict me, I did not think that Mnemosyne had seen snow in October within living memory. I had observed it in late November two or three times, but the present fall was beating that record by more than four weeks.

After the surprise came a measure of relief. The snow was relatively light, and it melted as soon as it hit the ground, which had not yet chilled to freezing point; it did not give the appearance that it would begin to accumulate significantly until I was safely ensconced in the Sprite. The molten snow was damp, of course, on my clothing as well as the road, but it seemed, at least to begin with, a discreet dampness far less annoying than the kind of abrupt soaking that substantial raindrops cause. The flakes were falling in clusters, but they were not dancing and swirling as snow inevitably does when the air is turbulent; they were all falling perpendicularly, in parallel, with an apparent military discipline that made them seem purposeful.

Then, too, the white snowflakes made the atmosphere seem a little less oppressive. It was not so much that the sky was so very gray, but the fact that the air itself seemed to have lost some of its quality, to have taken on a slight and strangely indefinable bad odor—a whiff of brimstone.

Given that I had spent the morning painting a scene set in a gloomy underworld, the poor light and oppressive atmosphere had not hindered me as much as they might have done had I been endeavoring to paint a cheerful portrait, and might even have seemed to collaborate with the effect I was trying to achieve, but the last thing I wanted was for the island to turn into an Underworld scene, in an effort to inspire me with a clearer notion of Hades' mythical realm than I had yet been able to conceive. That would have been taking the pathetic fallacy to ridiculous extremes, as well as being rather hard on all the other residents.

I was already striding out purposefully, so I could only have hastened my pace by running, and I was not about to do that, and more than I was likely to take up dancing, so I simply plugged on, estimating that I should not be too bedraggled when I reached the Sprite, and that twenty minutes standing in front of a roaring fire, turning round judiciously now again, should restore me to comfortable dryness, even if I were looking somewhat short of my best.

I did not realize quite how far short of my best I would look until I reached the outskirts of town, and used my right hand to brush away the snowflakes that were accumulating on my coat. Automatically, when I had cleared all that the hand could reach, and the fingers were beginning to feel numb with cold, I glanced down at it, wondering whether I ought to reach into my pocket for a handkerchief in order to wipe it dry.

The hand was dirty.

I am a scrupulous man, and I knew full well that my hands had been perfectly clean when I set out, and that my coat had been very carefully brushed—not by me, admittedly, but brushed nevertheless, and Jean-Jacques is as scrupulous as only the proudest of manservants can be. I could not, therefore, help leaping to a suspicion, if not a conclusion, that many people would have thought too absurd even to consider: that the snow, in melting, had made my hand dirty as well as wet.

Absurd or not, it was an easy hypothesis to check. I inspected my clean left hand, and then extended it, palm up, to catch a few dozen clusters of drifting snowflakes. Then I held the hand close to my eyes, and watched the snowflakes melt.

Each cluster, as it turned to water, left a sprinkling of tiny but unmistakable black dots on the skin, which looked for all the world like particles of soot.

"Black snow!" I exclaimed, aloud.

I was exaggerating: the flakes still falling around me looked perfectly white, no different from snow that I had seen falling hundreds of times before on Mnemosyne, though never in October. This time, however, *was* different; this time, the white flakes had black hearts, and the long celebrated similes "as white as snow" and "as pure as the driven snow" had suddenly taken on a delightfully ironic ambiguity.

The old proverb is true, then, I thought. *There really is always something new under the sun. Or, at least, under the clouds.*

I looked up as I added the rider. Dense cloud was still covering the entire sky, as dull, uniform and depressing as the stone paving of the ancient Temple of Minerva—the only deity whose desertion in recent centuries I sometimes regretted. No movement was visible in the clouds, because there was no contrast that could have revealed movement, but I had a strange sensation, perhaps due to some mysterious psychological quirk rather than the expertise of my painter's eye, that the vapor was nevertheless unquiet: that the wind that had dropped at ground level might still be blowing, lazily if not turbulently, in the strata of the atmosphere that humans and hawks can only reach in the nacelles of balloons.

The pathetic fallacy really did seem to be going over the top, in an ironic echo of my painterly endeavor—but I knew how ridiculously vain it would be to think that the climate of an entire region, home to tens of thousands of people, might change simply to reflect the artistic difficulties of one man, even a genius. Vanity I had, in the modest dose appropriate to my vocation and my image, but not the kind of vanity that leads to insanity. The fact that the gloomy weather had arrived, out of season, while I was endeavoring to represent the ultimate in gloom by imagining the realm of Hades, could only be a coincidence, a little irony of fate.

Whatever is driving this snow, however, I added, continuing my train of thought, *is definitely not pure.*

But I stopped myself then, lest I turn thoroughly Roman and begin seeing omens. We are supposed to live in an Age of Enlightenment, or even, some scholars insist, a "Post-Enlightenment" Era in which enlightenment is so taken for granted that no one any longer feels the need to boast about it, and would seem behind the times if he did. That, of course, is the view people take in the Capital, rather than Mnemosyne, where superstition still rules many of the minds that art does not, but the Capital sets the tone, and the intellectuals of Mnemosyne, do not like to seem any less Enlightened that the stalwart captains and pilots of Lutece.

Naturally, having never gone in for false modesty, I pride myself on being the most enlightened of them all, as a result of which, I could not allow myself to consider any natural event literally ominous.

One the other hand, though, *black snow!* If that couldn't qualify as an omen, what could?

Once again, I had to remind myself that the snow still looked white, the blackness not being at all evident while the flakes were still falling—but that hardly affected its qualification to be seen as an omen by anyone who was in the habit of seeing omens. Quite the contrary, in fact.

Omen or not, the circumstance seemed so extraordinary that I quite forgot that I had decided to walk to the Sprite in order to have an interval for meditation, in which I could take stock of my situation: a situation that was on the verge of commencing to seem ever s slightly uncomfortable. It was too early yet to suspect that I might fail in my endeavor, but things were not proceeding as smoothly as I might have hoped, and certainly had hoped when, being unusually short of requests for portraits and hearing the whisper of ennui stirring in the depths of my brain, I had accepted, at Myrica Mavor's urgent insistence, the Marquis de Mesmay's commission to paint a triptych illustrating the career of the mythical Orpheus.

Precisely because I had never done anything similar before, it had seemed an intriguing challenge, and I had had no doubt, when the Marquis and I shook hands on the deal, that I would rise to it heroically and meet it triumphantly. The thought that I might not be up to it had never entered my head.

Now…well, I still would not grant it official entry to my head, but the snagging suspicion had crept in anyway, through some unsuspected fissure in my supposedly-impregnable wall of self-confidence.

The very idea that Axel Rathenius might have accepted a painterly task that was beyond his artistic reach was, of course, as unthinkable as…well, as unthinkable as black snow… but still...

The fact remained that I had come out to walk to the Sprite—beneath a sky so dismal that any child or moron could have judged that *something* was likely to descend upon me before I reached my destination, even if only a lunatic could have offered an exact prediction—because I had wanted space to meditate on the problems of painting the Underworld, and I was not doing that. Indeed, I seemed to be doing anything but that, allowing myself to be distracted by Toustain's bequest, the gloominess of his former dwelling, and the eccentricities of the weather. Clearly, I was out of sorts, not quite myself. I had to shake it off, pull myself together…and above all, stop thinking in clichés.

For the time being, however, I used the back of my left hand to brush the dirty snow off the right sleeve that my right hand had, inevitably, been unable to reach. Then I reached into my pocket, very gingerly, to take out a handkerchief with which to wipe both hands.

Then, of course, I had a dirty handkerchief. There are some situations from which a fastidious man simply cannot emerge unscathed.

Fortunately, I had reached the Sprite. Before going upstairs I went into the tap-room in order to borrow a towel and a clothes-brush from the proprietor's wife, Madame Auger, who was at her invariable post behind the counter. While she went to fetch it I nodded a greeting to old Nicodemus Rham, who was sitting in a corner with a glass of red wine. There were half a dozen other men in the room I knew by sight, but no one to whom I owed a greeting. No one was taking about the weather, presumably because no one there was yet aware that it was snowing, let alone that the snow was dirty. My clothes, of course, were uniformly black; they did not show the snow because it had melted, and they did not show the sooty deposit it had left behind, because it matched them.

I tidied myself up as best I could before going upstairs to the upper floor, where I knew that Myrica's little reception party would be gathered by the bay window in the far corner, so as not to be far away from the fireplace, and asked the proprietress to send the serving-girl up with a hot toddy. Her eyes expressed the surprise that her mouth dared not express.

"It's cold outside," I explained. "We have bleak winter ahead of us, it seems."

Madame Auger nodded sagely. A bleak winter would not be bad for business, given that there was always a good fire blazing in the Sprite—two, if the upper room were in use—and when the nights became twice as long as the days, the humble folk of Mnemosyne still sought company, and still told tales around the fire, as if the Age of Enlightenment were something that only affected the upper stories of finer houses.

The fishermen, stevedores and domestics who formed the regular custom of the tap-room had a habit of referring to the first floor as "the summer palace," as if the mere presence of the occasional Lutetian aristocrat could create a palace out of bare floorboards and poorly-papered walls, and reduce a population of artists to the ranks of mere court jesters. Given that the one regular summer visitor possessed of real political power, the fearsome Duc de Dellacrusca, never set foot in the Sprite, the designation seemed more hopeful than appropriate.

II. Awkward Expectations

The members of Myrica's welcoming party were the only customers in the upper room, which made the smallness of their number even more glaringly obvious, even without the automatic contrast my own mind drew with the far more convivial tap-room,

Myrica had not been able to gather much of a court. Hecate Rain was there, of course, and the medium Vashti Savage, but there was not a single musician, or, for that matter any other painter. Even Fion Commonal, who remained an assiduous regular in the upper room in spite of the fact that he was always complaining that his medical vocation and duties as the head of the Island Council never gave him a spare minute, was absent, perhaps having found a bone to set somewhere on the far side of the island. There were only four chairs gathered around the table, and the fourth was occupied by Niklaus Hylne, a self-styled historian who considered himself the island's foremost antiquary since poor Ragan Barling had been sent to jail on the mainland for double murder and a few petty crimes of lesser esthetic interest. Perhaps he was, given that he had bought a substantial fraction of Ragan's collection, and had also been conspicuous by his presence and his disdain when old Toustain's effects had been auctioned off.

Meager as it was, it seemed that Myrica's reception committee was about to get even smaller, because I had no sooner stepped across the threshold than Vashti Savage leapt up from her seat and ran—literally ran— twenty-five or thirty paces to meet me. I had known Vashti, casually for nearly twenty years, but I had never seen her do anything so extraordinary before. She didn't even like me—some people don't, incredible as it might seem.

"Master Rathenius," she said, in a low voice, although we were far enough away from the trio who were staring after her in frank puzzlement for there to be very little danger of their overhearing, "may I ask a favor of you?"

"Certainly," I said, there being no danger at all in allowing people to ask for favors, as long as one has not promised in advance to grant them.

"Would you call on me tonight then, after you have greeted Master Parenot? It should not take long—a matter of minutes."

I glanced out of the window—perhaps a little too conspicuously—at the falling snow.

"I'll send my carriage back to pick you up," she said, immediately. "Robert can take you home afterwards. It will save you getting wet, as you obviously walked here."

I regretted that my attempt to tidy myself up had been so woefully unsuccessful. Whatever Vashti wanted to talk to me about was evidently something that required privacy, at least in her opinion. I had no reason to decline her request to call in on her, especially as it would earn me a lift home in a closed carriage. As for the favor, I could afford to wait and see...

"That's very kind of you," I said. "I'll call as soon as I can." I assumed that I would be doing Robert a favor too, as he would have two opportunities to put his feet up in the Sprite's tap-room for a while instead of one, and all for the paltry cost of driving me back to the headland—albeit after dark and in poor weather, in all probability.

Vashti went downstairs then. Obviously, she had not come to the Sprite in order to catch a glimpse of Charles Parenot, whose fame had clearly not spread as far as his loyal agent had hoped and believed, but simply because she knew that I would be coming. It was understandable that she had not wanted to come to my house, fearful of being turned away if I were in my studio. Jean-Jacques, being a perfect model of manservants, has a fine talent for superficially-polite rudeness that can send a chill down the spine of any but the hardiest of importuners.

I walked over to the corner table and took the seat that the medium had just vacated, where the hot toddy was soon placed before me. Everyone looked at it with polite astonishment. I repeated the explanation I had given Madame Auger, adding a remark about the seeming poor quality of the atmosphere, and the need to adapt medicinal alcohol to the specific requirements of circumstance.

"You really shouldn't have walked, Axel," said Hecate, maternally.

"On the contrary," I said. "It was an exceedingly fortunate decision. Had I come by carriage, I would not have realized so soon what a prodigy the snow is."

I was fishing, but I only caught an old boot.

"Utterly unheard of, snow in October," said Niklaus Hylne, taking entirely the wrong inference from my allegation of prodigy. He shook his head, sadly. "I've been here nearly twenty years, and I've never seen the like."

"Axel's been there longer than that," said Hecate. "Have you ever known it snow in October before, Axel?"

"No," I said, deciding to shelve the news about the black snow, which they clearly did not deserve to hear.

"How long *have* you been here, Axel?" Myrica Mavor put in, curiously. She had only been my agent for a few years, and had not qualified at the outset as a seasoned dealer of long standing—she never revealed her age but had to be younger than Hecate, and much younger than Vashti Savage—but she had obviously been familiar with my reputation before I had hired her, and had probably made sufficient inquiries into my previous career to suspect some mystery there.

"Longer than I care to remember," I said, with an artificial sigh.

"There certainly aren't many people who've been here longer," Hylne put in.

"There are hundreds," I corrected him, "if not thousands."

"I'm not counting the indigenes," Hylne said, unnecessarily. "I meant *us*."

His "us" was a bid to be considered part of our company: the company of artists. I could not think of many of us—my "us," that is not his—who would have considered him part of that select number, but artists are all egomaniacs, and mostly jealous so the assumed exclusion might not have been entirely fair. Niklaus was certainly an intellectual, as well as a relentless gossip, and a serious student of his history as well as a collector of curiosities.

"And where were you living before, Axel?" Myrica put in, blithely unaware of the fact that her curiosity, if taken much further, might cost her one of her most lucrative sources of commission.

Fortunately, everyone had their own train of thought to follow, and Hecate cut in before I could reasonably have been expected to come up with the answer I had no intention of providing.

"Axel isn't even the oldest of the incomers," she said. "I was talking to someone only yesterday who said that she remembered him arriving on the island—although she didn't say exactly when that was."

I assume that I was more surprised by that remark than anyone else, but I had no intention of following it up, curious as I was; I wanted to steer the conversation on to safer ground.

"How long will it be before Parenot's boat arrives?" I asked Myrica.

She didn't get a chance to answer either. Niklaus Hylne asked the question of Hecate that I had not: "Who was that?"

Hecate blushed slightly. That surprised me. She must have spoken thoughtlessly, not realizing that she was exposing herself—not that I could think of any plausible reason why she should be embarrassed about talking to someone old enough to remember me coming to the island, if anyone did. There might well, as I'd said, have been hundreds, or even thousands, of indigenes who had been here when I arrived, but I would have been prepared to wager that not one of them would have actually remembered my arrival, and I could not imagine that any of the "incomers" who might have preceded me would have had any reason to take note of my taking up residence, which had been accomplished without any publicity.

Hecate employed the same tactic to avoid answering the question that I had. She looked me in the eye and said, firmly: "How is the Orpheus coming along?"

She knew perfectly well how the accursed triptych was "coming along." As one of the very few people to whom my door was not barred, and who was even allowed into my studio, under the strict conditions that prevailed there, she had called in on me two days before, and offered me her commiserations when I explained to her why my progress was so slow that I was only part-way through painting the second panel, and had only sketched the third. Given that she knew that, and that she was supposed to be my closest friend, it seemed a trifle tactless for her to ask such a blunt question in compa-ny—especially the company of my agent.

"Very well," I lied. "It's slow work of course, be-cause I'm so very meticulous, but I think the Marquis de Mesmay will be very pleased when it's finished. I hope he doesn't intend to spent the entire winter on the island waiting for it, though—there's really no need for that."

"It's a good job he isn't here, then, to see you slack-ing," said Niklaus Hylne, smiling to indicate that it was supposed to be an amicable quip, not an insult. We had obviously embarked upon a competition of tactlessness. I had no intention of joining in.

"I did invite him," said Myrica. "I thought he might come—I've sold him three of Charles' paintings, after all—he even has one of them here on the island. Did he show it to you, Axel?"

"Yes he did," I said, rapidly, glad to be back on safe ground. "The man has undoubted ability. Although..."

I left the remark dangling, deliberately. Surely that hook wasn't going to be left unbitten.

"What do you man, *although*?" Myrica demanded, reliable as ever. "That's almost as bad as *but*. I know that painting—it's first rate."

"You're right," I said. "And I really didn't mean anything by the *although*. You certainly shouldn't think that I meant to imply anything unfavorable to Master Parenot. I'm not at all familiar with his work, but if his *Eurydice* is an accurate measure of his talent, he is, as you say, first rate, and you can be proud as well as glad to have him as client."

"Eurydice?" Hecate echoed, faintly—but so faintly that no one but me paid any attention.

Hylne was still determined to be tactless. "Perhaps it's as well that Monsieur de Mesmay didn't know that Parenot was coming to the island when he commissioned you to paint the Orpheus triptych, Rathenius," he said. "After all Parenot has a fine reputations as a mythological painter, while you're best known as a portrait painter—a portrait painter of genius, of course," he added, with suspicious belatedness.

"If Mesmay had wanted Parenot he could have had him," Myrica pointed out, scrupulously. "He had no particular reason for wanting the triptych painted on the island. He could have commissioned it in the Capital just as easily... even more easily, in a way..."

"I'm not so sure of that," said Niklaus Hylne. "From what I hear, Mesmay isn't delaying his return to the mainland simply because he's waiting for Master Rathenius to fulfill his commission—as Rathenius points out, there's no reason why he should do that. The word is that he intends to settle here permanently."

That was intriguing news, if true—although, given the general reliability of island gossip, it might be so much hot air. If the summer migrants were going to start settling, the island might be on the brink of another economic transfiguration.

"Why would he do that?" asked Myrica, bluntly, as if the very idea were insane. She often came to the island out of season to pick up paintings, but never stayed long, and didn't bother renting the cottage she routinely reserved for three months every summer, only taking a room on the second floor of the Sprite. The idea of being permanently resident anywhere but the Capital probably seemed quite bizarre to her, even though she knew full well, at some level, that the world was a big place and populated almost everywhere. For "her" artists, on the other hand, she thought the island was an ideal location. For such a hard-headed businesswoman, she had oddly romantic notions about what made artists tick.

"That's a mystery," said Niklaus, stressing the final word just sufficiently to make it clear that he meant something more than the trivial meaning of the word— not that anybody cared. At least, I assumed that nobody cared.

"You didn't answer my question," I pointed out to my loyal agent. "When is Parenot's boat scheduled to arrive?"

"It should be here by now," Myrica replied, looking out of the window at the harbor, which was conspicuous- ly empty of anything larger than the usual smattering of fishing-smacks. Parenot was supposed to be coming from the mainland in a lighter that had sufficient storage space in its hold for his luggage. Painters tend to have a lot of luggage, even when they haven't just bought a house whose furniture has all been sold off for the sup- posed benefit of the poor and needy.

"It's undoubtedly been delayed by the bad weath- er," Niklaus observed.

"It's not that bad," I observed. "The wind has dropped, and the snow is still relatively light. The sea seems calm enough, at present."

"It is now," Myrica agreed. "They might have been late starting out, though, and even if they weren't, there was a fierce north-westerly blowing earlier, which would have been directly against them."

"It was a bitter wind," Niklaus agreed. "Unusual, for October, and it had an uncommonly bad taste. It looks as if we're in for a ferocious winter."

Myrica was staring out of the window, evidently wondering where the lighter had got to, and perhaps beginning to worry already about the possibility of an accident that might cost her one of her best clients.

Hecate took the opportunity to lean closer to me and say: "What did Vashti say to you? It must have been very urgent, if she came here especially to see you."

"Don't you know?" I parried.

"No," said Hecate, innocently enough. "Which is odd, I suppose, as I'm her best friend and she doesn't even like you. Although, when we were talking about you before you arrived..." She shut up, obviously realizing that she had let her mouth run away with her again.

"Really? I said, lightening my voice to make a joke of it, trying to let her know that I wasn't going to hold it against her. "Doubtless you were complimenting my genius, and she politely refrained from opining that I had none."

"Not at all," said Niklaus. "We were just wondering why on earth the Cult of Orpheus might have commissioned you to paint an altarpiece for them."

That was really throwing a stone into the frog-pond. Hecate looked embarrassed and Myrica looked furious.

" So far as I know," I said, this time making my voice a trifle frosty," Monsieur de Mesmay has no connection with the so-called Cult of Orpheus, if it even has any real existence nowadays, and what I'm painting certainly isn't an altarpiece. As you say, had the adherents of any mystical religion wanted a work of art for ceremonial purposes, they would certainly have turned to one of their own members."

"Niklaus is just being mischievous," Myrica said. "Nobody was wondering any such thing—not even him, really. We were actually talking about the mystery of coincidences, although it isn't really a coincidence, is it, that Hecate is working on a poem about Eurydice while you're working on a set of paintings featuring Orpheus. You're friends, after all; she simply took her inspiration from you."

"Actually," said Hecate, "that isn't what..." This time, it wasn't her who abandoned the sentence; she was cut off rather rudely.

"I know who it was!" said Niklaus Hylne, abruptly. "Of course!"

He had lost us all.

"Who what was?" asked Myrica, mystified.

"Who the person was who remembered Rathenius arriving on the island, of course," said the supposed historian, although I couldn't see that there was any *of course* about it, and I would have much preferred him not to bring the topic back into the conversation. So would Hecate, to judge by her blush.

It was left to Myrica to say: "Who?"

"The Mother Superior," said Niklaus, triumphantly.

Myrica was unimpressed. "And who the hell is the Mother Superior?" she demanded—rather inaptly, given that Mothers Superior, of whatever religion, are supposed to be the least likely people to end up in Hell.

"Of the Convent of the Sisters of Shalimar," Niklaus added, considerably less triumphantly now that he had seen how direly underappreciated his power of divination had been.

Myrica looked at him as if he were mad. "I thought lay people weren't allowed into the Convent," she said.

The Sisters of Shalimar was a religious organization, of Druidic affiliation rather than Christian, although obviously founded in imitation of the Christian tradition of monachism. They were often to be seen drifting around in the distinctively voluminous cream robes and head-dresses designed to reduce them to anonymity, doing various good works—mostly helping to tend the sick who couldn't afford pay doctors, probably more effectively than most qualified physicians, if only because they administered no treatments, and hence did not compound the harm caused by malady or injury. I had never met the Mother Superior, though. As far as I knew, she never left the Convent, and men were not allowed to enter it, so opportunities for us to run into one another had been a trifle sparse. The prohibition did not, however, apply to all lay people, as Niklaus explained

"Women are allowed to go in to seek instruction in the mysteries of the Bardic tradition," Niklaus told Myrica, loftily, still trying to save some vestiges of triumph, "and rumor has it that Hecate has been taking advantage of that license quite frequently of late."

At the time, that seemed to me to be almost as ludicrous as black snow. Hecate Rain, thinking of going into a convent? Hecate Rain, thinking of going into a convent without *having said a single word about it to me*? Utterly absurd. It didn't occur to me immediately that there might be other reasons for a woman to go into a convent for "instruction" than consulting the Superior about joining the Order. As I have already remarked, I wasn't quite myself that day. The poor air quality was probably affecting my brain.

"Well, yes," Hecate admitted. "It was the Mother Superior." She conspicuously neglected to offer any explanation for her visits to the Convent—if, in fact, rumor was right in alleging that there had been more than one.

My resistance broke down, taking my wisdom with it; curiosity won. "Why were you consulting the Mother Superior of the Sisters of Shalimar about me?" I asked.

"I wasn't," she said, defensively. "She asked me."

"Asked you what?" I said, quite mystified.

"How your painting was coming along—the Orpheus triptych, that is."

Why on earth would she be interested? I thought— but my brain was catching up now, and I didn't ask the question aloud. It didn't matter, it was one of those questions so obvious that it didn't have to be voiced to saturate the atmosphere.

"It's not really surprising," said Hecate, still on the defensive. "She knows that I'm working on the poem about Eurydice, obviously..."

Obviously? I thought.

"...so she naturally asked me why," Hecate continued, letting that unspoken query pass, "but I didn't say anything about your painting. She was the one who brought the subject up, passing naturally enough from Eurydice to Orpheus. Obviously, she'd heard about the Mesmay commission, and she mentioned, in passing, that she remembered you arriving on the island. Then she asked me how the painting was coming along. She seemed really interested, and I didn't want to lie to her... she's a Mother Superior after all, even if her religion is dying... so I told her you were having difficulties..."

There went her mouth again.

"What difficulties?" Myrica snapped. "It's the first I've heard about difficulties. Didn't you say just now that everything was going very well?"

"It is," I lied. "Of course there are difficulties—what's worth doing if it doesn't present difficulties?—but I'm overcoming them. That's what art is all about."

It isn't but, unlike Hecate, I wasn't talking to the Mother Superior of a dying religion, and saw no reason to be absolutely truthful.

"So, you see," Hecate continued, not exactly valiantly, but at least with the substitute for courage that a desperate struggle to get out of trouble always provides, "there was really nothing to it… it was just casual conversation. And The Mother Superior isn't what you might imagine. She might be a mystic of sorts but she's a genuine scholar, of real intellect. She has a bigger library than yours, Niklaus, even now, and she's told me all kinds of things about the Orpheus myth that will be very useful for my poem; she knows a lot more about it than you do, Axel... and she's not the recluse people assume. She does go out sometimes; it's just that no one ever recognizes her, because no one on the outside knows who she is. You and she even have… or had… a common acquaintance, Axel, why is probably why she was interested enough to ask after you. She used to go to see the old woman on the mountain, the mad morpheomorphist, just as you did."

Eirene Magdelana had never mentioned the Mother Superior of the Sisters of Shalimar to me—or, if she had, I hadn't understood the reference—but why should she? Whereas, as a true egomaniac, I could think of any number of reasons why she might have mentioned me to any other visitors she might have had.

Hecate till hadn't explained, however, why she had been in the Convent of the Sisters of Shalimar in the first place. She obviously had no intention of doing that here, in front of Myrica and Niklaus—but I was enough of an egomaniac to think that she wouldn't keep it a secret from me, now that she had let enough slip to bait my curiosity. I resolved to go to see her the next day, if I could spare the time from my accursed commission.

Somehow, I didn't think that would be a problem.

III. The Image of Eurydice

I still felt damp, and uncomfortably aware of the invisible blackness that was insidiously dirtying my clothes, and I felt the need to dry myself off a little more rapidly, so I picked up my hot toddy and moved to stand with my back to the fire, muttering an apology.

Hecate and Niklaus automatically turned their chairs to face me, in order to include me in the continuing conversation, but Myrica, equally automatically, took another glance in the opposite direction first.

"There!" She stabbed a carefully-manicured finger in the direction of the gray gloom, which was even more intense out to sea. This time, in spite of the fact that the snow hadn't completely stopped falling, she had caught sight of a black dot somewhere in the white wilderness. I screwed up my eyes and concentrated, and eventually saw it too: a visible black particle, amid all the invisible ones sheathed by the snowflakes.

It was definitely a boat heading for the harbor, and it was not far off. I swallowed the last of my drink, set the cup on the mantelpiece, and edged a little closer to the table again.

"It's him!" Myrica added, although one black dot looks sufficiently like another, especially through a curtain of snow, for the one we could barely glimpse to be any kind of boat.

Convinced that it was the lighter bringing Charles Parenot and his luggage to the island, however, Myrica remembered yet another of the questions raised by left unanswered, and turned back to me. "You never did tell me what you thought was wrong with Charles' *Eurydi-*

ce," she said accusingly. "Come on, Axel, spit it out. Why did you say *although* when you agreed that it was a first rate painting?"

I sighed, remembering that I had wanted to draw the discussion away from my murky past when I had issued the provocation, but no longer feeling sure that I wanted to go down that road, especially if Master Parenot was about to make an appearance. This time, though, no one got in the way. Even Niklaus Hylne had run out of the tactless desire to stick his oar in.

"It is a fine painting," I agreed, "But it's just a picture of a pretty girl's head set against a dark background. When Mesmay showed it to me, I could see immediately that she's supposed to be a shade rather than a living individual, but I couldn't see why she's supposed to be Eurydice rather than any other shade of a pretty girl. It's not really a criticism of the artist, and I suppose it arises from the fact that I have exactly the same problem myself, and don't know how to solve it. The middle panel of my triptych depicts Orpheus charming the shades in Hades, and although we can infer that Eurydice is among them, there's no way of telling her apart from any other shade of a pretty girl. There's nothing in the myth by which to identify *her*, except in a painting that isolates her with Orpheus in a recognizable situation, as in the scene where he reaches the threshold of the Underworld and looks back—but that was excluded by the terms of the commission. Mesmay specifically asked for a depiction of Orpheus charming the shades. Crowd scenes aren't my forte anyway, so yes, Myrica, it posed difficulties... but I'm tackling them, with my customary artistry."

Myrica didn't seem satisfied, but it wasn't my explanation that was failing to satisfy her.

"He does use her rather a lot," she said. "Too much, in my opinion. But it's difficult for me to broach the subject diplomatically. *You* could mention it though, Axel... artist to artist and setting diplomacy aside. He's seen a lot more of your work than you've seen of his, thanks to my expertise in placing your work in the Capital. He'll respect your opinion more than mine."

"I'd probably be glad to help," I said, "or at least willing, if I had the slightest idea what you're talking about."

"He uses his wife as a model far too frequently," Myrica explained, succinctly. "No matter what his subject is, he tends to cast her in the part—and sometimes, as you say, there's nothing but the title he puts on the picture to indicate who she's supposed to be. It's in danger of becoming something of a joke, and affecting his sales."

Niklaus had got his second wind. "She's not his wife," he put in. "She's just a whore." He must have realized instantly, from the hostility of the three gazes that fixed themselves upon him, that he had gone too far. "A retired whore, I mean," he added, swiftly. The amendment did not reduce the malice of the insult or save the situation, and he actually made things worse by adding: "But once a whore...," before shutting up.

Myrica sighed. "What have you heard?" she asked, trying to make it clear that it was her professional interest in a client that was making her ask, not the kind of vulgar appetite for gossip that had evidently activated Niklaus Hylne's over-eager ears.

"It's an old story in the Capital, apparently," he said, slightly defensively. "The fact of his moving out has reactivated it, though. It's said that the girl who passes for their daughter was dumped on his doorstep one day, presumably by the mother, who must have thought, rightly or wrongly, that he was the father. He didn't have the heart to take the baby to the foundling home, possibly because he made the same assumption, so he took it in and tried to look after it. He was hopeless, and the girl who was modeling for his current painting—one of the whores from the Mount—volunteered to help. She moved in, and apparently gave up general whoring to become a full-time mistress... and substitute mother. The girl's too old to need much looking after anymore, but he seems to have got habituated to having her around, so, instead of using the move to the island as an excuse for breaking with her and leaving her on the Mount to resume her old career, he's brought her with him. He comes from a respectable family, it's said, albeit from Bretagne—ours, that is, not the islands—so there can't be any question of marriage."

"That doesn't exclude love," Hecate murmured, although no one else bothered to follow that train of thought.

"Is that all?" Myrica demanded—riskily, since it was a virtual confession that there was something else to know, which Niklaus would become avid to discover, if he didn't know any more already.

Apparently he didn't. "Why, what else is there?" he demanded.

"Nothing," said Myrica. "All right, so far as I now, that story's not so very wide of the mark—but it's completely irrelevant. Charles and Mariette live together now in perfect respectability. The past is dead, gone, erased. The fact that they've never made any official registration of their relationship is neither here nor there, and it ought to matter less on Mnemosyne than anywhere else in the province, or the Empire. There's no call whatsoever for any sniggering behind their backs, and I certainly hope that there's no one on the island who would stigmatize the child for the fact that she was a foundling. She's perfectly charming—Axel will love her, just as he'll love Mariette, and he'll want to paint them both—and Elise is a talented musician, quite the child prodigy."

As a professional agent and skilled saleswoman, Myrica was a dedicated enthusiast, never shy with her praise, so I took her assurances about my feeling an instant urge to paint both the mistress and the adopted daughter as soon as I clapped eyes on them with a pinch of salt. I only hoped that she hadn't fed the child's ego with too much talk of her supposed potential. A man of my age can cope with the conviction of being a genius, but it's the sort of idea that can throw a child seriously off balance.

"Oh, yes," said Niklaus, as if he had just remembered something. "There was *that*."

"What?" Myrica demanded, impatiently.

"Nothing," he said, paradoxically. "It's said that Parenot is something of a fiddler, and that he's taught his... wife and kid too. Learned it from a wedding-fiddler back in the sticks, apparently—an old lunatic who told silly stories. You know what Bretons are like with their fanciful tales. Nothing damaging... except... well, the word is that it has something to do with him having to leave the Capital... the fiddling, that is. Nobody knows what, exactly..."

The black dot was now quite obviously a lighter. It had passed the harbor entrance and was maneuvering to dock at the quay. The snow had eased considerably, and it was possible to see three passengers standing on the deck, motionless among the busy crewmen. They were looking toward the shore.

I screwed up my eyes again, trying to make out their faces, but they all had the hoods of their gray cloaks pulled up, and the snow, light as it was, still distorted my vision sufficiently to make it impossible to discern any detail. It was obvious that they were a man, a woman and a child, though, and easy enough to imagine that they were looking up at the lighted window on the first floor of the Sprite, able to see us limned by the glow of the lamps that Madame Auger was in the process of lighting, even though nightfall was some way off. Perhaps, I thought, all three of them were wondering whether we were looking at them, and what, if so, we might be thinking.

I was looking at them and wondering, but Myrica was still looking daggers at Niklaus Hylne, wanting to clear the air of slanderous taints before her client arrived.

"Charles plays the violin," she was telling him, sternly, "purely for relaxation. He taught Elise to play, but she's overtaken her teacher now. She has a natural ability that he lacks. That has nothing to do with his decision to leave Martyr's Mount. I've been recommending strongly that he move here for some time, because I'm convinced that he'd benefit from a change of scene, and that the island will suit him as much as it suits Axel. When the Toustain house came up for sale, I told him it was too good an opportunity for him to miss, and I finally managed to persuade him that it was a logical step in his career, now that he's on the brink of major commissions. I've got a big client lined up for him, and he was kind enough to back me up on the suggestion."

"Who's that?" I asked, interested.

"I don't want to say until the deal is firm," she told me, shaking her head. "It might jinx it." She wasn't talking superstitiously; she meant that if the potential client found out that she'd been bragging about the commission while it was still only a possibility, he might be annoyed.

"Anyway," she went on, still addressing Niklaus. "It will do Charles and Alex good to be close together. A little competition between artists always stimulates the inspiration. He's a great admirer of your work Alex, obviously, and he's looking forward to meeting you."

So there it was, exactly as I'd hypothesized. Myrica had been urging Parenot to make the move for some time, because of her silly notion about the stimulating effects of rivalry—except that, now she had voiced it, I no longer believed that that was the only reason for the move. There was something she wasn't saying: something she'd been afraid that Niklaus Hylne might have heard on the mysterious grapevine that carries scurrilous gossip all round the world. But what?

I was as intrigued now as Niklaus—even more so, in fact. And unlike him, I had a perfectly legitimate reason to be interested in the hidden motivation of a fellow artist, just as I had a perfectly legitimate reason to want to know why Hecate Rain was visiting the Sisters of Shalimar. Or so, at least, I told myself.

While Myrica went down to greet Charles Parenot on the quayside, I stayed by the fire. Hecate and Niklaus remained in their seats. We had volunteered to go with Myrica, of course, but half-heartedly, and she had assured us that there was no need for us all to expose ourselves to the snow. She assured us that she would bring her guests up directly, as soon as she had ordered a large pot of freshly-brewed tea and a bottle of brandy.

When she had left the room, I turned my attention back to Niklaus Hylne. I had a bone to pick with him.

"Why did you suggest that the commission for the triptych came from the Cult of Orpheus?" I demanded, curtly. Because I was standing and he was sitting I had a positional advantage that backed up my authoritarian tone. It had its effect

"Mesmay's said to be a member," Niklaus retorted, defensively.

There was no point in asking by whom. Who can ever tell where such rumors start? I continued to exercise my illusory authority.

"Because he collects works of art associated with the Orpheus myth?" I said scathingly. "That's not evidence of membership in a secret society. I've never heard any mention, during my time here, of the active presence on Mnemosyne of either of the surviving mystery religions. There isn't even a strong Druidic presence, except for the Sisters of Shalimar."

"Well, you would say that, wouldn't you?" Niklaus retorted, resentfully as well as defensively.

My jaw is not in the habit of dropping, but it nearly made an exception. I held it in place. "Are you saying that the vicious old fools who feed you your ridiculous fantasies think *I*'m a member of the Cult of Orpheus?" I said.

"No," he said, trying hard not to be intimidated and not succeeding. "Quite the opposite."

Since time immemorial, the two principal mystery religions that the Romans had inherited from the Greeks before the advent of the Divine Julius had been thought to be at war. The Orpheans, it was said, believed that Dionysus had ordered his maenads to murder Orpheus. The Dionysians denied it, and claimed that the accusation was a slanderous fabrication—but they would say that, wouldn't they? I could see that if my image were taken a little too seriously by certain people, I might be suspected of Bacchic tendencies, but I had always thought that my best and most obvious feature was an ironic skepticism that would rule out any suspicion of religious affiliation. I realized, though, that the reason that Niklaus had earlier expressed surprise that Mesmay had commissioned me to paint the Orpheus triptych was not that he supposed me to be an infidel, but that he suspected that I might belong to the enemy camp.

"It's ridiculous, Niklaus," I said, in perfectly level tone. "Mesmay is an art collector, not a secret fanatic, and I'm an artist. I don't say that we're two of a kind, or that either of us knows the other particularly well, but we're both intelligent men—and Mesmay's wife is reputed to be a spiritist, which probably wouldn't sit well with being married to an Orphean, even if the cult is nowadays just another club of conspirators and back-scratchers, which long ago lost any connection with the faith of its founders. You can't seriously believe, either, that I'm involved with the Cult of Dionysus?"

"Toustain left you his books," countered Niklaus.

I hadn't seen that one coming.

"You're saying that Toustain was a Dionysian?" I queried, almost laughing at the implausibility. "He was the last man in the world I could imagine consorting with Maenads, or even getting seriously drunk."

"Appearances can be deceptive," Niklaus insisted. This time, he was less defensive. He was surer of his ground. Something he had seen or bought at the auction of Toustain's assets? No—it had to be something that he'd got from the notary, Guillot, who still had Toustain's papers. As a notary, Guillot was still supposed to be maintaining confidentiality in their regard, but I hadn't formed a high opinion of his professionalism when I'd been invited to call on him to receive the good news about my unexpected bequest. Apparently, the man of law felt that, since all the interested parties were dead, his lips didn't need to be so tightly sealed. It wasn't surprising that he was Niklaus Hylne's notary too—an artists' colony isn't the kind of place that brings notaries flocking like hungry vultures, so the choice is limited. But Monsieur de Toustain a follower of the Cult of Dionysus? I couldn't believe it, even though the first rule of being a member of a secret society is to maintain that secrecy.

"There is absolutely nothing among Toustain's books to suggest that he was a Dionysian," I said, firmly, racking my brains in the attempt to figure out whether I was telling the truth. Although I hadn't unpacked the crates on to shelves, I had looked through the books to see if there might be anything among them of particular interest to me. They weren't old, for the most part—they certainly didn't include any manuscripts or incunabula— and I hadn't noticed anything very esoteric, or that I knew to be rare. There were books on various religions and mythologies, but they were popularizations or scholarly treatments, such as could be found in any decent library.

"Perhaps not," said Niklaus, unrepentantly, "but the word is out that he was—and you were the only person on the island he ever talked to, and he did leave you the only bequest he didn't abandon to the island's poor. You can't blame people for wondering."

In fact, I could—but for the moment, I didn't have to. Myrica had reappeared at the top of the staircase, accompanied by two hooded figures: a petite woman barely out of her twenties and a girl, no more than twelve or thirteen. They had both pushed back their hoods to reveal a striking study in contrasts. The woman was thin, with pale blonde hair, an ideal model for a shade, but the girl had black hair and a robust frame, seemingly bursting with health. No one could possibly have taken them for mother and daughter.

I had to issue a mental apology to Myrica; she had judged me more accurately than I thought. As soon as I looked at the pair of them, partly because of the striking contrast in their very different kinds of beauty, I wanted to paint them—not just because they were beautiful, but because their beauty was interesting, even intriguing. As an expert judge, I very rarely find beauty mysterious, but there was definitely something covert in the anxious eyes of the pale Mariette, and something indefinable in the gaze of the girl, who was also afflicted by a very understandable timidity on coming into a strange environment for the first time, but who gave the impression of not being fundamentally timid at all. She was only a child, as yet, but she was on the threshold of a nascent maturity, and she might well be already becoming aware of the power that her beauty would give her—especially if she were being lavished with praise by the likes of Myrica Mavor on account of her supposed musical talents.

But where was Charles Parenot?

"Charles wouldn't come up," said Myrica, obviously not pleased by the fact that her plans had gone even further awry—although, given the woeful inadequacy of the welcoming party, she could have reckoned it a mercy if she had put her mind to it.

"You must excuse Charles," the blonde woman out in, scanning us all with her pale eyes, the irises of which were turquoise, tending more toward green than blue. "He's terrified of what the porters might do to his precious paintings, and he won't let them out of his sight. He won't be entirely sane again until they're safe in the house and no one can touch them but him. He doesn't mean to be rude."

Myrica seemed to be too busy seething to make the introductions, so I gallantly stepped into the breach. "There's no need to apologize, Madame Parenot," I said. "You husband is entirely right to put his works of art ahead of mere social convention. I too am a painter, and I understand perfectly. Axel Rathenius, at your service. This is my dear friend Hecate Rain, the poet, of whom you must have heard, and this is Niklaus Hylne, a noted historian. I'm sorry that we aren't a larger crowd, but the weather has turned unusually nasty, and artists are notoriously sensitive to the cold."

While I was jabbering, Myrica had at least had the decency to pour the tea and the brandy, so the lovely blonde now had a cup in one hand and a glass in the other, while the equally lovely ingénue was holding her warm cup in both hands.

"Thank you, Axel," said Myrica. "And this is Mariette"—she indicated the blonde—"and Elise."

There was a confusion of inclined heads that might have passed for bows in more aristocratic company.

"I must admit," said Mariette, "that I hadn't realized, when Charles decided to move here, that the island would have such a remarkable climate. Snow in October! And such strange snow!"

I was the only member of the welcoming committee who knew what the last remark meant, and I smiled at the advantage. "It isn't typical, I assure you," I said, "And I'm truly sorry that elements are conspiring to give you such a poor first impression. In fact, it's the first time in living memory that it has snowed here in October, and so far as I know, black snow has never fallen here before."

"What do you mean, black snow?" asked Hecate. "It looks white to me."

I was about to explain when I was struck by the curious expression on the little girl's face, which seemed to be a reaction to the mention of black snow, although I couldn't quite make out whether it was fear or fascination. I had been observing her mother, having seen her blush very slightly when I had called her "Madame Parenot," but I had sufficient peripheral vision and more than sufficient peripheral attention to keep them both in view.

"There's no need to be alarmed, my dear," I said to young Elise. "The snow is an oddity to be sure, but you and I have both been exposed to it, and it hasn't done us the slightest harm, has it? It's just a freak of nature."

I was right, of course, but not everyone is as stern as I am in their refusal to believe in omens. Who could blame the poor child, uprooted from the heart of the capital and brought to an island that must seem to her to be remote, only to be greeted by black snow?

She made no reply, but looked back at me as if she were trying to weigh me up, not having decided yet what to make of me. I hoped that I would come out of the inspection well. I looked to her mother-substitute for support, but I realized that, in spite of the porcelain rigidity of her features, she was definitely suffering from an unease that was more intimate than any reaction to the strange quality of the local snow.

Whatever Myrica had not told us about the Parenot household's reasons for leaving Paris, I guessed, they were not as mundane as she had tried to make out. I resolved to interrogate her about it when I got the chance. I would doubtless find out if I did get the opportunity to paint them both, but I could not think about that seriously until I had finished the Orpheus triptych, which might take some time.

"What do you mean, black snow?" Hecate repeated, plaintively. I owed her an answer, but for the moment, I felt an odd desire to give the woman and the child a better welcome than Myrica and the weather had contrived to arrange.

"As Myrica has doubtless told you," I said, addressing both of them, "I'm your nearest neighbor on the promontory where your new house is located. You'll be able to see my house when you get down from the cab at your new home—you can't mistake it. With your permission, I shall send my manservant, Jean-Jacques, and my cook, Luzon, to your house tomorrow, in order to help you settle in. I shall refrain from importuning you while you are still in the process of sorting things out, but I shall call the day after—again, with your permission—in order to pay my respects to your husband. If there is anything you need, please don't hesitate to ask Jean-Jacques; he'll be able to find anything you might lack."

"You're very kind, Master Rathenius" said Mariette. "Can we give you a lift back, if you don't have your own carriage? We'll have plenty of room—Charles will undoubtedly insist on traveling the cart with his paintings and equipment—but at least I'll be able to introduce you to him when we get there."

"Thank you," I said, with genuine regret, "but I've agreed to visit someone when I've finished here, and she promised to send her carriage to pick me up."

Hecate looked at me in surprise yet again, even though she must have deduced readily enough that it was Vashti that I had agreed to visit, and Robert who would be waiting downstairs with a carriage to convey me to her house. It was, however, to Mariette that she addressed herself.

"If you have no objection," she said, "I'll gladly accept the place that Axel can't take up. My house isn't very far out of your way, and the carriage in which I came"—she shot a meaningful glance at me—"is apparently otherwise occupied."

"I would be glad..." Niklaus Hylne began, but Mariette got in ahead of him.

"Oh, please do," she said to Hecate. "I'd be very pleased to make your acquaintance. Myrica tells me that we have something in common, since you're writing a poem about Eurydice. I posed for Charles' depiction of her."

"So I understand," said Hecate. "I really must obtain an invitation to visit the Marquise de Mesmay, so that I can see it. I know her socially, of course, but I've never been to her home."

"Is it here, then?" Mariette asked, taken by surprise. "I had assumed that it was in the Capital."

"Monsieur de Mesmay has commissioned Axel to paint Eurydice too," Myrica put in. "I believe he brought your husband's picture here in order to show it to him—by way of inspiration." She was being slightly mischievous. Again, Mariette had blushed slightly at the mention of the word "husband," but again she had no intention of issuing a correction.

"Only as part of a triptych dealing with the mythical exploits of Orpheus," I hastened to add to Myrica's comment. "Eurydice will only appear in one panel, in a crowd of shades. But I would be delighted if you would sit for me some time in the near future for an individual portrait—as yourself, not as Eurydice."

"Myself?" Mariette echoed, in a tone that suggested that her self could not possibly be of any interest, by comparison with the various roles in which her husband cast her.

I had already turned my attention to Elise. "And with your permission," I said, still putting to an appearance of addressing Mariette, "I would love to paint a portrait of your daughter. She's a talented musician, I hear—perhaps I could paint her playing the violin. It would make a beautiful study."

I am not in the habit of trying to seduce girls as young as Elise, but even though I had no hidden agenda, I was delighted with the way that the girl's face lit up at the suggestion. The equivocation disappeared from her expression, and she was suddenly confident. Presumably, she was no stranger to being sketched and painted, but there is a world of difference, for a child, in being sketched and painted by one's father and sitting for a portrait by the foremost portraitist in the province. She did not, however, express her enthusiasm verbally.

All that Mariette said was: "That's really too kind, Master Rathenius."

She meant it literally; she really did think that I was going too far. I resolved to be more subtle in my future flattery. I had no hidden agenda with the regard to the lovely Mariette either, in spite of what Niklaus Hylne's venomous tongue had alleged about her morals. I was fully prepared to regard her as a faithful wife, if only for reasons of professional courtesy. I do have a reputation, though, that goes beyond painting, and she might not have been aware of the fact that I really do paint a great many portraits simply for the pleasure of... well, not simply painting, but of simply seeing and understanding, without even attempting any earthier physical interaction.

Niklaus added his assurance of willingness to help, confident that no demand was likely to be placed on him, and that allowed Hecate to make a third attempt to clear up the mystery that was still nagging away at her.

"Why did you call the snow black?" she asked me, for the third time.

"Because the crystals appear to have formed around nuclei of soot," I said. "When the snow melts, it leaves dark stains behind. If I were not wearing black, and these two ladies had not draped themselves in voluminous gray cloaks to protect them during their crossing, you would be able to see the evidence."

"Soot?" Hecate queried. She was wearing pale blue, and looked down anxiously at her silk blouse,

"Apparently," I said. "I suspect that there must be a fire somewhere on the island, which has combined its smoke with the low-lying clouds." Even as I said it, it sounded ludicrously inadequate as an explanation for such a large scale phenomenon—but what other explanation could there be?

"That's the prodigy you mentioned when you arrived," Hecate said, belatedly catching on. I could see that it was on the tip of her tongue to say that she hoped it wasn't a bad omen, but she stopped herself, and glanced sideways at the little girl. She didn't want to worry the child with a careless remark that might be taken too seriously. I smiled to thank her for that, although she probably didn't understand the significance of the smile, and I wasn't entirely sure why I was thanking her. I took a deep breath, intending to steady myself, but even inside the Sprite, the air seemed heavier than usual, and it really did have a bad taste.

Something is happening, I thought, *and I don't know what it is*.

And I couldn't help reflecting that a refusal to believe in omens wouldn't prevent them from manifesting themselves, if there really were such things.

IV. The Haunted Medium

Mariette, judging that she and Elise had warmed themselves up sufficiently, and that they had done all that they could to respond to Myrica's misfired gesture of welcome, made their apologies and took their leave, wanting to start the difficult business of settling into their new home before nightfall. There were more smiles and reassurances, and I think they really did go away feeling considerably more confident than when they had arrived, even though the snow was still falling indolently, and still presumably hiding its secret blackness. Hecate went with them, and I had every confidence that she would put them further at their ease, and would make a friend of Mariette.

"It could have been worse," I said to Myrica, when the three of them had gone.

"Really?" she said, although she knew that I was right.

"Eurydice is truly charming," Niklaus opined, attempting subtle provocation.

"Yes she is" I said, "but from what Hecate has shown me of her poem, she doesn't quite fit *her* image of the woeful nymph."

"Too blonde?" Niklaus suggested.

"Too... composed."

"Unlike her daughter," he suggested, although he was following up his own judgment rather than responding to mine. "If I didn't know that she was a musician, I'd suspect that one might grow up to be an Amazon."

"You shouldn't have said straight away you wanted to paint her, Axel," Myrica said. "You worried her mother."

"If I did," I observed, "it's because you haven't given her a sufficiently accurate portrait of me. I'm not an ogre."

"She's not her daughter," Niklaus reminded us—but was quick to add: "That's obvious just by looking at them. She must take after her father."

"Actually, no," said Myrica. "Not really—not at all, in fact..." She conspicuously didn't add: *If he is her father...* She didn't want to add fuel to Niklaus' malicious gossip.

"Well," I said, "I've done my duty and I must be going. Don't worry about the commission, Myrica—difficulties there might be, but nothing that true genius can't handle. Mesmay will be satisfied... eventually... and my reputation will not only be intact, but broadened. Next year won't be as lean as this one... especially if I can contrive to overcome Mariette's unjustified suspicions and paint that divine child entranced by her music."

"I think you're confusing her with Orpheus," said Niklaus, trying once again to be witty and failing dismally yet again.

"There's no danger of that," I assured him, while I made my exit and headed for the tap-room. Robert did not seem overjoyed to see me, having obviously made himself comfortable while waiting.

I nodded once again to Nicodemus Rham, still in his corner and still on his own. I was tempted to linger for a few minutes and exchange a few words with him, but I was curious to know what favor Vashti Savage wanted to ask of me.

She lived in town, so it was only a five minute drive. While Robert fed and watered the horses, without unhitching them, because he had to keep them in readiness to take me home, I rang the doorbell, and was immediately admitted to Vashti's drawing room by her kitchen-maid.

"Thank you for coming, Axel," she said. It wasn't the first time she had called me by my first name, but it wasn't usual.

"It's no trouble," I said. "You'll be doing me a favor if the weather gets any worse—it wouldn't be pleasant walking back to the headland if the roads have turned to mud and it's pitch dark. It's good of you to lend me Robert and your carriage."

She got straight to the point. "I understand from the constable that you've sometimes helped him in the apprehension of criminals by making sketches from the descriptions of felons given by victims."

That took me by surprise. I hadn't known what to anticipate, but certainly not that.

"Have you been the victim of a crime, Vashti?" I asked her, as delicately as I could.

"No," she said, blushing.

"Ah," I said, coming to what seemed to be the natural conclusion, given that she made her living as a medium, supposedly channeling the communications from the spirits of the dead for the benefit of the living. "I didn't realize that you had visions as well as hearing voices."

The principal reason why Vashti didn't like me, albeit not the only one, was that she knew that I was a skeptic. Although I had never accused her of being a charlatan, she was well aware of the fact that I did not put the same interpretation on her artistry as she did.

"It's true that I don't usually see the souls that communicate with me," she said, "but in this instance... you'll probably consider it to be nothing more than a recurrent dream, and I'm willing to admit that you might be right, but still, it is recurrent, and vivid, and I can't help thinking that it's an attempt to communicate, made by someone who can't, for the moment, find her voice. I want to help her, if I can."

I was genuinely interested, all the more so as she had made the effort, for once, to concede that she really didn't know what was happening to her, or what its significance might be.

"And you think that externalizing the image that you see in your... vision might help with that?"

"Yes. If nothing else, it will help me focus my own mind, which tends to go adrift when I'm entranced if I can't concentrate. And then..."

"You hope that one of your clients might be able to recognize the spirit in question, so that you'll discover who it is that is trying to communicate... which would be half way to deducing *what* it is they want to communicate?"

"Exactly. I knew you'd understand, even though you don't believe."

I made a slight apologetic gesture. "It's not that I don't believe *you*, Vashti—it's just that you and I put different interpretations on what it is that you hear... and see. I don't doubt that your experiences are real, and meaningful, and I'll be happy to help if I can. Do you happen to have a sketch-pad and charcoal in the house? I don't have mine with me."

She did—and had them ready to hand, having anticipated the necessity.

"She, you said?" I queried. "It's a woman, then. How old, would you estimate?"

"Thirty, perhaps—no older."

"Can you give me an idea of the general shape of her face: round, thin...?"

"Lean and delicate… a trifle meager, but naturally so, not starved. I don't think she's a pauper. Fair hair, by the way, and pale eyes—green, I think, although you won't be able to indicate that with charcoal..."

I drew a few tentative lines, questioning her about the adjustments that needed to be made, and we proceeded in a fashion that, without quite becoming routine, I had practiced a number of times, not just for Constable Clovis in the service of the law.

We had not even got half way through the procedure before I was struck by a strange suspicion. My hand began to move more rapidly, and I did not have to dirty it any further by wiping away incorrect lines. I finished the sketch in record time, with a remarkable alacrity, and used a damp cloth to clean the excess charcoal from my hand.

Vashti was suitably amazed.

"How did you do that?" she said. "You must have been reading my mind. You seemed to know what I meant while I was still groping for the right words to express it."

"I'm an artist," I told her. "Tell, me, Vashti, have you ever held a séance at the Marquise de Mesmay's house? I believe I've heard that she has an interest in spiritism."

"Twice," Vashti conformed, "but that's not a member of her family. Aethne asked me to try to contact her mother, who was in her sixties when she died."

"Did you hold the séances in the small reception room?"

"Yes—the big one's practically a ballroom, far too large for something as intimate as a séance. Why?"

"Did you happen to look at the portrait hanging over the mantelpiece?"

"Portrait?" She was catching on, and her expression took on a hint of resentment that was quite unjustified. "I vaguely remember there being a picture, but I have no memory at all of what—or—who it was."

"Not consciously," I agreed. "But you did see the portrait, twice, and your memory did record it, even though you can't summon up the memory in your normal state of consciousness. When you're asleep, on the other hand..."

"A portrait!" Vashti repeated, uncertainly. "I suppose... but how could you possibly know? How could you recognize it from the vague description I was giving you. I hadn't even contrived to bring it into proper focus in my own mind."

"I had help," I admitted. "I was looking at the face in question less than an hour ago, and quite intently, hoping that I might get the chance to paint it myself. As soon as I realized the direction in which your description was heading, it was easy to complete it."

"But you weren't in the Marquise de Mesmay's house an hour ago... surely you were in the Sprite."

"Yes, I was—and so was she... not the portrait, but the model. Her name is Mariette. If you'd waited for Charles Parenot's boat to arrive, you'd have seen her yourself, and you would have recognized her instantly."

"But that's impossible!"

"I can assure you that it isn't, and I'm certain that you'll have a chance to prove it soon enough. Hecate is befriending her as we speak, and she'll certainly introduce you to her when the opportunity arises."

"But she's dead!"

"She is, I can assure you, very much alive. There's not an atom of doubt about it."

Vashti seemed quite agitated—more agitated, in fact, than the situation seemed to warrant. Reluctant as she might be to admit that she had made a mistake, and that the image that had appeared in her dream was that of a portrait, rather than one of the dead souls who employed her, as she saw it, as a means of communication with the living, she had no grounds for doubting what I was telling her—the speed with which I'd completed the sketch was proof enough that I too had seen the image that had come to her repeatedly in her sleep.

"She's dead, I tell you!" Vashti insisted. "I *know* it."

I thought I understood, but I knew that I had no chance of convincing her with the aid of reason. I had never experienced it myself, but I knew that people who have visions sometimes acquire, along with those visions, an unshakable conviction that what they've seen, no matter how improbable it might be, is true and indubitable. It must, I knew, be a matter of some physiological trigger in the brain, some mechanism that attached faith to certain items of belief, and set them beyond doubt. On such psychological stuff are the foundations of religions based—and the fact that such visions sometimes produce flatly contradictory accounts, making it logically impossible for them all to be true, or even very many of them, the logic in question is impotent to defeat the faith that each visionary has in his own vision; whatever has happened in the mysterious depths of the brain has made such doubt literally impossible, on the part of the visionary.

There was, therefore, nothing extraordinary, in principle, in the fact that Vashti's vision of Charles Parenot's Mariette had come with an attachment of the conviction of her demise, even though I had seen her in the flesh and blood, alive if not quite entirely well, less than an hour before. And what I had said to Vashti was undoubtedly true: Hecate Rain would introduce the two of them, when she had the chance.

I was not sure that Vashti, always a rather highly strung individual—as mediums tend to be—would come through that encounter unscathed, if she retained her unshakable conviction that the image in her dream was someone deceased. I wanted to shield her from the effects of the seeming paradox. Even if she didn't like me, she was a friend of a friend, and I ought to help her if I could. But I couldn't do that with logic. It would need art.

"I think I can see where the confusion arises," I said, in a voice as soft and soothing as I could contrive. "You and I are looking at this from different angles, as usual. Yes, there *is* a sense in which the image you saw is dead, and in which the person your unconscious mind is trying to channel—whatever we can mean by that—really does belong to the spirit world... very much so, in fact."

"What do you mean?"

"I mean that I've seen the model, but that you've only seen the portrait, and the portrait specifically identifies the image as a shade, not merely by the artistry of the representation, but in its title. Parenot is a mythological painter, and in this instance, he painted his wife as

Eurydice... perhaps the most famous of all the shades in Hades, according to the relevant mythology."

I wasn't expecting effusive gratitude, necessarily, but not was I expecting her to look at me as if I were a scorpion that had just crawled out of her shoe. I realized, a trifle belatedly, that substituting a fictitious character from mythology for a living individual wasn't necessarily an advance, from the strict spiritist point of view.

I hastened to paper over the crack.

"We have no idea what the real Eurydice looked like, of course," I said. "If she appeared as herself, given that she seems to be unable to speak, how could she make her identity known? Whereas, by adopting the appearance of a portrait—a portrait that you had seen—she had an opportunity to be recognized. And it worked. You needed a prompt from me, but you did work out who it is that has been trying to call herself to your attention: not Mariette Parenot, but Eurydice herself."

I didn't believe a word of it, of course; I knew perfectly well that there had never been a "real Eurydice" and that she was a fiction, a work of art in every sense of the term—but that didn't mean that Vashti couldn't believe it, if it gave her a lifebuoy to grasp while she was in danger of drowning in paradox.

She was hesitant, but that meant that the battle was half won.

"You don't really believe that I'm channeling Eurydice, do you?" she challenged, suspiciously.

A simple yes would have been too blatant a lie. I had to hedge. "Why not?" I said. "In my way of thinking, it makes perfect sense."

"What do you mean?"

"Well, as you know, I don't believe that there is a literal Underworld, or spirit world, in the sense that the myth of Orpheus and the faith of spiritism represent them, but I do believe that there is meaning and significance in the ideas. You think of me as a skeptic and disapprove of me because you think that means that I must consider you a liar or a fool, but that's not the case. I believe that you do experience what you say that you experience, and that even though the images come from within you rather than without, that doesn't mean that they don't have anything valuable or interesting to communicate. If we can set aside for the moment the question of whether your interpretation or mine is the correct one, we can examine the truly interesting questions that arise, and the ones to which you quite rightly and very reasonably want answers: Why Eurydice? Why now? And what is she trying to communicate you, albeit in silence?"

Although I say it myself, it was a very clever deflection, and it did, indeed, succeed in focusing her attention on the three questions with which I'd concluded the speech—which really were the interesting ones, for me as well as for her.

"Not quite in silence," she said, by way of amendment.

"Oh?" I queried.

"She doesn't speak—but she sighs."

"Ah," I said. "Lamentation, then?" In Hecate's unfinished poem, though, the lamentations of her Eurydice were much more voluble.

Vashti knew that too. "She's not like Hecate's vision of her," she said, tacitly accepting, at least for the time being, that it really was Eurydice who was trying to get in touch with her from the Other Side. "She's too..."

"Composed?" I suggested.

Again, I wasn't expecting gratitude, but the venom in the glance she shot me seemed far too excessive for such a harmless suggestion.

"You do know, don't you," she said, waspishly, "that Hecate's poem is really about you?"

That was a surprise too. I blinked. "What do you mean?" I queried.

"That it's not really Eurydice's lament that she's pouring into the poem but her own."

So I was being cast as Orpheus now. It was better, I supposed, than a Bacchic consort of maenads... although there was something of the maenad about Vashti, for the moment, and even Hecate had her moments...

I wrenched my train of thought back to the matter in hand. "Did she tell you that?" I asked, skeptically.

"No, of course not—I'm not even sure that she's conscious of it, but it's obvious."

Not to me, I had to admit—and, indeed, I couldn't believe it. I shook my head, which was enough to annoy Vashti again. Obviously, doing her the favor that she'd steeled herself to beg from me hadn't made her any better disposed toward me.

"You do know that she loves you?" she shot at me.

"Of course—just as she knows that I love her."

"Not enough to marry her." Another surprise. That was Vashti's own idea too; I was absolutely certain that Hecate Rain would never have told her that she had the slightest desire to marry me.

"I love her enough *not* to marry her," I told her. "It's not the case that good friends make good spouses. Hecate and I have been lovers in the past, but neither of us felt any inclination to perpetuate a circumstance that both of us, by virtue of our essential nature, can only experience ephemerally. You've misinterpreted the poem, Vashti. Of course Hecate's own feelings are entangled with her version of Eurydice's lament, but I'm not what she's regretting. If you'd waited until the poem was finished, you'd have understood that."

"Have you seen the ending, then?"

"No, because she hasn't written it yet—but I understand Hecate, better than you do, I believe, and I know, at least, where it *isn't* going. I'm not her Orpheus, and if I were, it wouldn't make any difference, because that's not the real substance of her lament. I can't speak for your Eurydice, obviously, or for Charles Parenot's, but I can speak for hers."

I refrained, of course, from pointing out that Vashti was projecting her own lament into Hecate's, and reading it as an allegory of her own existential plight rather than her friend's supposed predicament—with the crucial amendment, of course, that it wasn't my failure to embark upon a more committed and exclusive relationship that Vashti was regretting, but Hecate's. Hecate was her Orpheus, and had been for a long time, although I wasn't entirely sure that Vashti had admitted that to herself, let alone anyone else.

I understood and sympathized, of course. I didn't love Hecate in quite the same way that Vashti did, but I did love her, and I could understand perfectly how someone else could. What's more, I could do that without being jealous—unlike Vashti, obviously.

Vashti tightened her lips, but she forced herself back to the matter in hand, from which she'd allowed herself to be drawn away at a tangent.

"What do you think the answers to your questions are?" she said, this time with a marked lack of venom, because she really did want help in figuring it out.

"Why Eurydice and why now don't really seem that mysterious, given that the character is on everyone's mind at the moment—but perhaps that's too simple. Myrica thought that Hecate had started her poem because I'd taken on the Orpheus triptych for Mesmay, but Hecate denied it. She hasn't even seen Mesmay's Parenot, so she didn't get the inspiration there either, and there's no connection, so far as I know, between Parenot's decision to take up residence on the island and Mesmay—Mariette didn't know that the Eurydice was here rather than in Paris. Thus, we're dealing with a pattern of coincidences rather than a manifest chain of cause and effect—which doesn't, of course, exclude a hidden chain of cause and effect whose links we can't yet see. As to what your Eurydice is trying to communicate to you…well, if it's your unconscious mind trying to shove something up to the level of consciousness, you might have to work that one out for yourself."

"And if it's not?" She meant: *what if there really are supernatural forces at work?* But there are no "supernatural forces"—there are only natural ones that lie temporarily beyond our artificial and blinkered conception of the natural, which will become perfectly understandable if and when we can obtain the right data on which to build our theses.

"I don't know," I said, in order to be on the safe side. "Let's await further developments, shall we?"

At least, I thought, *she won't have a heart attack when Hecate introduces her to Mariette. Forewarned really is forearmed in that instance, and it was an exceedingly fortunate inspiration on her part to ask for my help—not that she seems to be fully appreciative of the good I've done.*

63

"I'd better go home," I said. "It's beginning to get dark, and although it's not a long journey, I don't want poor Robert to have to make his way back in a nocturnal blizzard."

She accepted that excuse. She had enough food for thought now without subjecting me to any further interrogation or accusations. So had I.

V. Threat and Mystery

I thanked Robert sincerely for driving me home, and gave him a good tip. As he maneuvered Vashti Savage's carriage around in order to head back to town I put out my right hand to catch a few clusters of snowflakes, in order to ascertain whether they still had black hearts, or whether that tiny measure of abnormality had stolen quietly away.

It hadn't. The melting snow still left tiny black particles on my palm. I peered at them more closely, trying to make out some kind of detail, but they were too tiny.

I nearly jumped out of my skin when a voice close to my right ear said: "Master Rathenius?"

The twilight had almost faded away, but Jean-Jacques had set a lamp over the front door, as he always did when I was out after dark, so I was able to make out the features of the youth who had spoken.

"Tommaso?" I said. "You scared me half to death. Where's Lorenzo? What are you doing here?"

The questions lacked logical order, but not logic. The one thing one always wondered on seeing one of the Dellacrusca twins was where the other one might be, since they were usually inseparable. The mighty Dellacrusca had returned to the mainland four weeks previously, as he always did when the end of his "vacation" fell due, always taking his unruly sons with him; Tommaso and his brother should have been raising their particular brand of hell in the Capital, or enduring one of their father's legendary punishments.

"I need to tell you something," Tommaso Dellacrusca muttered.

It was then that I realized that he must have been there for some time, waiting for me. He was wet and cold.

"Come inside and get warm," I said, as soon as the door opened. "Why didn't you wait for me inside?"

"I did ring," Tommaso said, directing a reproachful glance at Jean-Jacques, "but your man wouldn't let me in."

Sometimes, Jean-Jacques can be a little too strict in his duty, and it had to be admitted—even by Tommaso—that the Dellacrusca twins would not be high on anyone's list to obtain instant admission to a house in the absence of its master.

I set out to repair the damage: "Tommaso needs some hot soup and a glass of brandy," I told Jean-Jacques. "Is there a fire in the drawing-room?"

"No sir. You didn't..."

"I know, I know—but there is one in the studio, at least?"

"As always, sir."

"Good. Bring the soup there. Take Tommaso's coat to the kitchen to dry by the stove, and fetch him one of my mantles. I need to talk to you before I go to bed, by the way—important matters."

"Yes, sir," said Jean-Jacques, dutifully, looking at Tommaso almost as reproachfully as Tommaso had looked at him.

I put some extra logs on the fire in the studio, and stoked it up. Then I sat Tommaso down in a chair beside it and studied the condition of his trousers. They were dirty as well as damp, but it wasn't his fault.

"What do you need to talk to me about, Tommaso?" I asked—and added, because it seemed a natural question in the circumstances: "Has something happened to Lorenzo?"

"Yes, sir," the boy replied, unconsciously picking to Jean-Jacques' manner of address to go with his carefully respectful tone. "I don't know quite where to begin..."

"At the beginning," I suggested.

He nodded his head, as if acknowledging wise advice.

"Yes sir. Well, sir, as you know, Lory and I have... something of a reputation."

"Indeed I do," I agreed.

"And you won't be surprised, I suppose, to know that it's even worse in the Capital than it is here, where we're old enough now to pass for real bravos... apaches, they call them on the Mount and in Bellevue, but my father always says bravos, so that's how we think of it. Not that we *are* real bravos, you understand... if anyone does, you do... but we do like to give the impression... to pose, I suppose you'd call it..."

"I do understand," I assured him.

"Well, the thing is, three days ago we were out on the Mount, having a good time, and we were a bit drunk—not very, but enough. We'd been in a bit of a brawl—nothing serious—and we slipped away afterwards into a tavern where we thought no one knew us, needing to lie low. Except that somebody there did know us, and might have been following us, because this fellow comes to sit down with us, and buys us a drink, and then asks if we know the island of Mnemosyne.

"Well, obviously, we want to be seen to know what's what, especially when we do, so we assure him that we know Mnemosyne like the backs of our hands. And then he asks if we know a way of getting from the mainland to the island and back again without anybody knowing—and of course we do, because we've done it dozens of times, so you could say that we're past masters at it… and that's what we told him.

"Then he asks us whether we'd like to earn a little gold—he specified gold—by showing him the way, and giving him a helping hand getting across and back, so we naturally said yes we would. And then he buys us another drink, and tells us that he has a little business to do on the island that isn't exactly legal—which we'd already worked out, of course—and that he could do with some help. So we, naturally enough, ask him what kind of help, and he says, the kind that's paid for in gold.

"That was good news, of course—or so we thought—so we asked him for more details. He was tentative, as you might expect, but he tells us that it's a matter of a robbery, and that although he doesn't intend or expect anybody to get hurt, he might have to take some time looking for what it is he wants, and that it would be necessary in the meantime to keep the occupants of the house quiet—bound and gagged, that is—maybe for a couple of hours, and make sure that they didn't get up to any mischief.

"So we, naturally… or maybe not naturally, but it seemed so at the time… ask him how many people we're talking about and are they the kind of fellows who might be difficult to handle, and he, probably by way of flattery, says that two lusty lads like us could certainly take care of it, especially with a couple of good American revolvers to threaten them with, and that the number involved would be three.

"Well, we asked him to name a fee, and he did, and it seemed rather tempting—Father, as you know, although he's as rich as Croesus, tends to keep us on what he calls a tight rein, money-wise, and we were drunk…

and anyway, to cut a long story short, we said that we'd do it—and then, which was obviously the wrong way round, but we weren't quite thinking straight, we asked whose house it was he wanted to burgle, and he said it was yours."

I had seen that punch-line coming for some time, but he paused expectantly, so I said: "Ah!" in order to encourage him to continue.

"Well, Master Rathenius, that put us in a bit of a quandary, as you can imagine. I mean, of all the people on the island, you're the only one who's ever treated us half way decently. I won't say you've encouraged us, except for that one time when we rather let you down, but you've always seemed more amused by our pranks than disapproving, and once or twice you've even supported our stories when you knew full well we were lying, which takes guts when you're talking to Father, who isn't a man you want to get on the wrong side of...."

He was right about that. If ever there was a man one did not want to be on the wrong side of, it was Dellacrusca. He was reputed to the most powerful man in the province, and the nastiest, both of which reputations I was willing to believe, having had various dealings with him during his summer visits. I'm not easily intimidated, but he could send a chill down my spine with a glance. He didn't like me—or any artist, apparently. I had no idea why he came to Mnemosyne for the summer, although he'd certainly helped to make it fashionable with highly placed people. Perhaps it was a conveniently remote place to discuss the darker aspects of provincial security in relative peace.

"Go on," I said to Tommaso.

"Well, the long and the short of it is that we told him we couldn't do it. We weren't nasty about it, and we apologized, but we said that you were the one person on the island that we couldn't do a bad turn to, and certainly couldn't hold at gunpoint while we tied you to chairs and let some Italian thug ransack your house. I don't say there aren't people on the island that we could and would have done it to, but not you. I mean, when I came up behind you in the dark just now, you knew right away that it was me and not Lory. Even Father wouldn't have known that. You're the only man I know who can tell us apart. So no, I wasn't going to help him rob you."

I had painted the Dellacrusca twins—the only commission that the rich but somewhat miserly Dellacrusca had ever deigned to give any of the island's artists, thanks to one of Myrica's little miracles—and I had studied them with all my usual intensity as well as my gift. They'd been a good deal younger then, but I could still tell them apart at a glance. It wasn't really a compliment, but I was perfectly prepared to let Tommaso think that it was. One can never have too much moral credit with people who like to cultivate the image of being bravos and practical jokers.

"He seemed to take it in good enough part," Tommaso continued, "and he didn't get nasty any more than we had. He left, and so did we—only, when we're on our way home, and maybe a little unsteady on our feet, but not helplessly drunk, as we're crossing the street, this carriage comes hurtling out of nowhere, straight at us. Lory manages to push me clear, but because he thinks of me before himself he can't get out of the way, and the horse knocks him down, and the wheel runs over his leg. Broken tibia—not that serious, apparently, but he won't be able to walk for weeks.

"We thought about telling Father, who would have turned the city upside down looking for the fellow, and I certainly wouldn't have wanted to be in his shoes if he found him, but some of the hell he'd have raised would surely have rebounded on us, so we decided to let him think that it was just an accident—except that we figured that I'd better get out here as fast as humanly possible, to warn you that someone has it in for you. Without us, of course, he won't find it quite so easy to find a way to get back and forth from the island without any inconvenient indiscretion, but it's not that difficult. It won't be as easy for him to find his way around if all he's got by way of hired help is a couple of thugs from the Mount and some local fisherman he's recruited in the tap-room of the Sprite… but all things considered, he's not likely to be more than a day or two behind me.

"Anyway, I had to come—and after what happened to Lory, you can be absolutely bloody certain that if the bastard wants to get to you, he's going to have to go through me to do it, so two thugs won't be enough, even if they do have fancy American pistols. I know that you can handle yourself, and your man looks like a scrapper, so between the three of us, we should be able to hold the fort. What do you think?"

I had a great many thoughts, but I wanted to get them in order before I discussed them with Tommaso, so I left him to eat the soup that Luzon had warmed up for him while I went to have a word with Jean-Jacques. Rapidly, I told him what Tommaso had just told me.

"Shall I recruit extra troops, sir?" was his immediate reaction.

"No," I said. "I don't want a war, I want to know what the hell is going on. I don't think anything's likely to happen tomorrow, but I was going to ask you and Luzon to go over to the old Toustain house anyway, to help the new owner move in. We'll stick to that; it'll make certain that Luzon's out of the way, and you'll still be within easy reach if I need you back here. The other thing I wanted to talk to you about is a rumor I've picked up about Toustain. Apparently, Guillot—that's the notary looking after his affairs—has let something slip that he shouldn't have. Have you heard anything?"

Jean-Jacques was not an islander himself, but in the twelve years he had been in my service he had made a lot of friends and acquaintances, and the servants' gossip circuit is always more reliable than the ones to which Niklaus Hylne belonged.

"I have heard it said that Toustain wasn't his real name, and that if word of who he really was had got abroad while he was alive, he would have been in trouble—not with the law, apparently, but something worse. The Cult of Dionysus has been mentioned, although I'm not sure it even exists any more, although the other one certainly does. I can fish for more details, but you know what notaries are like, sir—they love to tease, dropping hints one by one. You might get more out of him by confronting him."

"I doubt it," I said. "Direct pressure would make him clam up. His is a profession that thrives on prevarication and procrastination. Find out what you can—and thank you."

"Do you want me to acquire one of those American pistols, sir? Just in case?"

"No. I don't want any shooting. First of all, I have to figure out what on earth it is that this mysterious individual wants to steal, why he thinks I've got it, and why he hasn't simply offered me the gold he's apparently willing to shell out in order to get his hands on it."

In order to do that, or at least to make a start, I went back to Tommaso, who had finished the soup and was sipping his brandy while warming his stockinged feet in front of the grate.

To begin with, I thanked him warmly for the trouble he'd taken to bring me the warning, and expressed my regret for what had befallen his brother as a consequence of his scruples. Then I got down to business.

"Did this mysterious Italian give you any idea of what it was he wanted to steal?" I asked.

"No. One of your paintings, I assumed."

"Not if he thought he might have to spend several hours searching. The likelihood is that it's something I've acquired recently, and could, in principle, hide away. How do you know he was Italian? Did he speak to you in Italian?"

"No, but he had an accent. I've only been to Italy once or twice, but Father used to live there before he married Mother and set his mind to taking over the province He still has lots of Italian friends and he's always jabbering away with them, so I'm familiar with the accent—it was odd, though, not Roman Italian. Venetian, maybe? I don't know."

Venice, I thought, was where *real* real bravos came from. But the would-be burglar had wanted someone with local knowledge—hence the Dellacrusca twins. Local knowledge and reputedly no scruples... but how was he to know that the twins, in spite of their image and reputation, had a few, specifically in respect of my person?

Silently I thanked the mischievous inclination that had always caused me to approve of at least some of the terrible twins' antics.

"Right," I said. "First of all, we're going to try to make a picture of this enemy I didn't know I had. You describe, I'll sketch, and between the two of us, we'll get a picture that we can give to Constable Clovis."

"The Constable!" said Tommaso, alarmed. "I don't want any of this getting back to Father!"

"I'll keep your name out of it," I promised. "Nobody needs to know that you were ever on the island."

I fetched a sketch-book and repeated the operation that I'd carried out earlier in the day with Vashti Savage—with much more difficulty, given that Tommaso had been at least half-drunk during his encounter with the Italian, and I had no convenient resource that would allow me to help him out. We ended up with a portrait of sorts, but I wouldn't have bet money on it being a good enough likeness to permit recognition if I happened to bump into the man who wanted to rob me.

"Right," I said. "I'll make a couple of copies later. Now, we have to get to work."

"What work?" Tommaso asked.

"We have to find what the Italian wants to steal. Once we have it, we can make a decision about what to do next."

"How are we going to do that?" the youth asked.

"We're going to go down to the library, and we're going to search very carefully through the three crates of books that Monsieur de Toustain left me in his testament. There's no way to be sure, but weighing up the timing and various other coincidences, the likelihood is that there's something among them that escaped my attention when I looked through them hastily on the day of their delivery."

"I'm not sure that I'd recognize a valuable book if I saw one," said Tommaso, uneasily.

"It might not be the book itself," I said, "but something hidden inside one."

"You man a secret message—a cryptogram?"

I suspected that the only books Tommaso and Lorenzo had ever read, at least outside the classroom, were vulgar thrillers. They had probably been as good a training as any for the vulgar thriller that he and I now seemed to be living.

"Something like that," I agreed.

We went down to the library and I showed him the three crates. "Let's take the books out one by one and leaf through them," I said. "If you see anything that seems unusual, let me know."

I assumed that I would have to check them all myself eventually, but he needed something to do while I worked. The kindest thing might have been to put him to bed, but it wasn't that late yet, even though he must have had a hard day.

"I don't suppose," I said to him, by way of making conversation, "that you've ever heard mention of the Cult of Dionysus?"

"As it happens, I have," he said. "Father says they're the scum of the earth, and ought to be exterminated."

For the second time that day, my jaw had to resist an almost-irresistible temptation to drop. "Lord Dellacrusca told you that the Dionysians are the scum of the earth?" I queried.

"Well, no," Tommaso admitted. "He didn't exactly tell me. In fact, he didn't know we were listening. It was one of his secret meetings. He's always having them. We used to make every effort to listen in, secretly, but it wasn't worth the trouble. They were always boring—incomprehensible, for the most part. The only interesting thing, really, was that his club is at daggers drawn with the other one you just asked about. And I don't mean daggers drawn metaphorically—I mean that it's a real feud, murders and all."

I presumed that he was exaggerating, but even so... Dellacrusca, an Orphean! Not, I presumed, in any religious sense—if ever there was an utterly godless man it was Dellacrusca—but in the more modern sense that the "cult" functioned as a kind of conspiratorial elite, dedicated to securing and holding on to as much political power as possible by the occult mans available to them; which, in their case, presumably meant stilettos and skullduggery rather than prayers and incantations. I recalled that Jean-Jacques had been certain about the continued existence of the Cult of Orpheus, even though he had been dubious about the survival of its legendary rival. If he was aware of some presence on the island...could that possibly explain why Dellacrusca, Alectryon and their cronies in the Peerage had taken to vacationing here? Were they holding meetings of what Tommaso called their *club*?

"That Dionysus fellow was supposed to have murdered one of theirs," Tommaso explained, helpfully, "but it was way back when, before Julius and the Empire. I don't think it's a real vendetta—just jockeying for lucrative posts in various administrations. There are more than two sides in that competition, on course, but the only ones that Father's friends really hate like poison are the Dionysians."

That didn't seem to me to be good news, given that the rumor seemed to be oozing around that the pseudonymous Toustain had been a secret Dionysian, and that I was one too. But if that was why someone wanted to rob me, it was hardly likely to be an Orphean who's tried to hire the Dellacrusca twins covertly to help him do it—not if Dellacrusca was himself an Orphean. On the other hand, if Dellacrusca was active in the political wing of whatever secret society considered itself to be keeping the Orphean torch alive, it didn't seem quite so ludicrously unlikely as it had when I had scoffed at Niklaus Hylne's suggestion, that the Marquis de Mesmay might be an Orphean too, and that his interest in possessing a symbolic triptych wasn't purely that of an art lover.

"*Merdre*," I said, suddenly overcome by the suspicion that I might have accidentally got myself into the middle of a contest whose crossfire might be dangerous. I cursed Toustain for his seeming generosity. What on earth had he been thinking? Had he realized that his real identity was bound to leak out after his death? Had he wanted to prevent whatever it was he was hiding from going up for auction with the rest of his worldly gods? If so, then why not simply bury the damn thing? Why drop it into my lap, without warning?

But I was getting ahead of myself. It was all wild conjecture. There might not be a single word of truth in it—apart from the overheard remark that Lord Dellacrusca had made about the Dionysians, which might only mean, now I came to think about it, that he was a high-ranking member of the Emperor's secret police, dedicated to wiping out all conspirators, of whatever notional stripe. That seemed more plausible, on reflection. It was far easier to believe in Dellacrusca as a secret policeman than an Orphean... except that appearances, as Niklaus Hylne had scrupulously pointed out, can be deceptive, especially when people are trying hard to deceive...

There was, after all, no contradiction in terms in thinking that Dellacrusca might be the leader of the secret Cult or Orpheus as well as the province's political police, and one could even argue that it might be a convenient functional combination.

In the meantime, I was going through the books as carefully as I could. There were no pieces of paper slipped between the pages. The books were all relatively recent, none more than a century old and very few more than half a century. There were dozens of books on religions, including Christianity, Judaism, Druidism, Mithraism, and the syncretized rites of Zeus-Jupiter-Amon and Minerva-Athene-Isis as well as the Greek Mystery Cults, but as I'd told Niklaus, they were all scholarly histories and commentaries, or popularizations of such studies for general readers. There were a handful of supposedly sacred texts, but nothing esoteric. Some of them were handsome volumes, with fancy binding and high-quality engravings, but they were just trade editions, easily purchasable even on the island, where almost all of them seemed to have been acquired. There were other history books, including some on the history of art and architecture, and a few works of philosophy, science and geography. No fiction or poetry at all. Some of the texts were in Italian, but most were in the vernacular.

"There's nothing here," said Tommaso, after each of us had inspected every single volume. There weren't that many—only a hundred in all.

"Seemingly not," I agreed. I examined the crates in which they had been packed. They were just crates.

"There isn't anywhere to hide anything," said Tommaso. "Except..." He picked up one of the few demi-folio volumes, and weighed it in his hand speculatively.

"Except what?" I said.

"Well, the covers are quite thick. If we're looking for a piece of paper, it might be inside.

I looked at the binding of the volume carefully. It was, indeed, sturdy, and it was not impossible that there might be an extra sheet between the thin leather surface and the board on which it was mounted—but I checked the spine first, as that seemed to be the likeliest hiding place.

I checked a lot of spines; there was nothing hidden inside them. If there was anything hidden in the bindings, it had to be laid flat on the board, underneath the surface sheet.

I checked all the demi-folio volumes, very carefully, and selected out the likeliest candidate.

"If we're wrong," I said, "we're about to ruin a work of art."

Tommaso didn't care. "Go ahead," he said.

I slit the binding. There was nothing hidden within it. So much for my judgment of likelihood. I slit two more, and only ended up ruining two more works of art. Works of mass-produced art, admittedly, but still, there was an element of uncomfortable sacrilege involved.

I was on the brink to giving up when I hit gold—or, to be strictly accurate, parchment. It was *very* artfully concealed, by someone who had gone to a great deal of trouble to do so, and if it hadn't been for the fact that the likely size of a hidden document had made the demi-folio and quarto volumes far more probable hiding-places than the octavos, a searcher who had no idea what title to look for could easily have gone through three-quarters of the volumes without finding the right one.

I took the utmost care extracting the piece of parchment from its niche without inflicting any further damage upon it than the slight nick I'd made in making the initial slit. Then I studied my prize.

"You were right," said Tommaso, meaning that he thought that *he* was right. "It's a cryptogram."

The parchment was full of strange symbols—more than a hundred and thirty in total, arranged in sixteen lines—not one of which was recognizable in the context of any written language I had ever seen. They might not have been letters or ideograms at all, in fact.

"How do we decode it?" Tommaso asked.

"I haven't the slightest idea," I admitted.

"What are we going to do, then?"

"First of all," I said, "I'm going to make copies of it—two, at least."

"That's not going to be easy," Tommaso said. "Those squiggles are very intricate.

The "squiggles" were, indeed, very intricate—but I'm an artist, and I have a very reliable hand and eye. It would be difficult at first, but as my mind adapted to the script, if it really was a script, my hand would become more fluent. Assuming that I could make do with two or three hours of sleep, as I often do when working with real intensity—successfully, provided that I don't attempt it too often in the course of a week—I hoped that I could, indeed, make at least two, and perhaps three adequate copies before daybreak.

"It's going to take some time," I admitted to Tommaso, "But I can do it. Then I'd like you to do me a big favor, if you're willing."

"Will it put one over on the Italian?"

"I hope so. That's the purpose of the exercise."

"Count me in, then."

"There might be some risk."

"Good." He meant it. He was giving every indication of spoiling for a fight. Coming here to warn me had apparently been step one in paying the debt of vengeance that he thought he owed his brother, but it wasn't enough to set his mind at rest. He was wound up, ready for action. It was probably a good idea to give him something to do rather than accepting his offer to help me "hold the fort."

"I'm not sure that there's anyone on the island at present who might be able to help unravel this," I explained to him, "although there are a couple of people that it might be worth trying, and I shall. In the Capital, on the other hand, there are real scholars of ancient scripts. I'll give you the name and address of one; if he can't decipher it himself, he'll surely know someone else who stands a better chance—and if there's anyone at all who can read it, he'll winkle him out eventually. You'll need to be careful, though. Someone's apparently willing to go to a lot of trouble to get their hands on this. They might not like the idea of copies being distributed hither and yon. I'll be as discreet as I can be, but if someone with an interest finds out that you have a copy in your possession, and are attempting to decipher it, you might be in danger of something worse than a broken leg. Until we know what this is and who wants it, there's no way of knowing what lengths they might go to in order to get it."

"Tell me where it has to go, and I'll get it there," Tommaso promised, firmly.

"Good," I said. "You'd better get some sleep now, while I make the copies. The sooner you can make a start in the morning the better. Can you get back to the mainland without delay?"

"Without anyone but you being any the wiser," he assured me.

I was probably the only person on the island who would have trusted a Dellacrusca twin with any kind of delicate mission, especially after what he'd just told me concerning the results of his eavesdropping on his father, but it seemed to be a worthwhile gamble, and it would get him out of the way—which anyone sane person would have wanted to do, given that he was the very model of a loose cannon.

"I'll get to work now," I said. "Tomorrow will be a busy day, given that we can't assume that your man will be long delayed in getting here. We need to make sure that even if he arrives tomorrow evening, he'll find that it's too late to get what he wants, no matter how many bravos and revolvers he has."

"You'll be running more risk than I will," Tommaso pointed out, scrupulously.

"Good," I said. It seemed the least I could say. There are times when one has at least to pretend to play the hero.

VI. Spreading the Word

My first visit, the following morning, was to Constable Clovis, who was always up with the dawn, and liked October more than June for more reasons than one. I gave him the sketch, and asked him to show it to his men.

"You can't arrest him," I told him. "He hasn't committed any crime on the island, and nothing provable in the Capital, but if he turns up here, it's because he's bent on mischief."

"If anyone spots him, I'll have him watched," Clovis assured me, probably glad of the chance to ask something definite of his men, in a season when there was usually something of a lull in the crime rate.

"He speaks with a slightly odd Italian accent," I told him. "Possible Venetian."

Clovis nodded. He didn't ask me how I knew about the mysterious stranger; like many of the indigenes, he was half-convinced that I was something of a sorcerer, and I had given him more help in the past than merely making sketches from descriptions given by his witnesses.

Niklaus Hylne was by no means as early a riser as Clovis, but his manservant was conscientious, and he went so far as to provide me with chocolate and bread fresh from the local bakery while he went to rouse his master and get him dressed.

Niklaus finally appeared.

"What is it, damn it?" he demanded.

I gave him the copy of the mysterious cryptogram.

"What's this?"

83

"I haven't the faintest idea," I told him. "That's why I'm here. You've been swollen up with pride in being the island's foremost antiquarian since Ragan went to jail, and you contrived to skim off the cream of his collection when it was sold off. Now it's time to take responsibility. You need to search your books for some clue as to what this is. I'm not asking you to read it—just to figure out what language the symbols belong to, some clue as to how they might contain meaning."

"Need?" Niklaus queried, not nearly as willing to pitch himself into the game as Tommaso Dellacrusca or Clovis. "I don't *need* to do anything of the sort."

"*I* need to know what this is, and as soon as possible," I told him. "My need isn't your need, admittedly—unless you value my respect and friendship. Do you?"

Niklaus was fully awake by now, and he stared at me hard.

"Ragan Barling would have jumped at the chance to show me what he could do," I told him, refraining from adding that Ragan had valued my respect and friendship so much that he had tried to poison me.

"I suppose expertise carries a certain responsibility," he conceded, and was quick to add: "Does this have something to do with the Cult of Orpheus... or the other one?"

"Yes," I said forthrightly. "It's the secret that the man who called himself Toustain was hiding. Since that idiot Guillot has let his real name slip, there seems to be something of a competition to acquire it. You're the first person to lay eyes on it, except for me, in at least twenty years, perhaps two hundred or two thousand. I'm a painter, not a scholar, so there's nothing I can do with it. I'm sending a copy to the Capital, but you have a head start. If you can get to the answer before the finest scholars in the world..."

That was more than sufficient bait to capture his attention fully. He raised the paper on which I'd copies the symbols as scrupulously as humanly possible to his eyes, and peered at them intently.

"I've never seen anything like them before," he said, although it was hardly news and didn't help.

"But you have Ragan's books now, as well as the ones you spend half a lifetime accumulating," I reminded him. "If you don't think you're up to it, or aren't interested, there's one other person on the island I can try."

I reached out my hand, utterly convinced that it would remain empty. It did. Niklaus even moved the piece of paper away, in case I tried to snatch it.

"Who?" he asked.

"I came to you first," I reminded him. "You're my best hope—but if..."

"All right," he said, feigning a world-weary compliance. "Since you're so insistent, I'll try."

"It's urgent," I told him.

"I can see that," he snapped. "I'll do my best. I can't promise anything."

I knew that. I left him to it. I had no great hope that he might find something, but he did have the best library on the island now... or the second best, if Hecate Rain's judgment could be trusted. I was prepared to trust it, at least in the absence of anything more solid.

By the time I got to Hecate's house, the sun was some way above the horizon. Even so, she was still in bed. I didn't have to kick my heels in her drawing room, though; I still had access to Hecate's boudoir, although—or rather because—the only thing we did there nowadays was talk.

I watched her take off her night-dress and begin putting on her underwear, admiring the contours of her thighs and hips. She was still beautiful, even though her face was showing more evidence of age than she would have wished, and I was still able to obtain a full measure of artistic appreciation from the texture and movements of her body as she clothed it delicately in silk. I had painted her five times, but never in the nude; her nudity had always been a private appreciation. Once, the appreciation had been confused by lust, but we were past that now, and it was far purer, in esthetic terms. I could have made love to her of course, and enjoyed it thoroughly, but I felt no animal urgency to do so. It was primarily as an artist that I savored her appearance and her odor, and primarily as an artist that I loved her—no less deeply for the quietude of animal lust.

As soon as her most intimate areas were covered, white she was still making her selection of outer garments, favoring dark garments for a change, in case it snowed again, she interrogated me with her gaze. I showed her the piece of paper on which I'd made the second copy of the symbols of the parchment—or the third, if the one that Tommaso Dellacrusca was already transporting across the continent in the direction of the Capital were reckoned to be the first, as it was probably entitled to be.

"What's this?" she asked.

"I don't know," I told her. "It's a secret. The late Monsieur de Toustain thought it important enough to warrant burying himself away as a hermit for the last decade of his life and more, and didn't want it to go up for auction with the rest of his paltry belongings. Why he left it to me, I don't know—perhaps because he's hidden it in the binding of a book and he figured that the best place to hide a book is in a library. He knew I had one, of sorts, and probably wasn't in a position to compare its size with any of the others on the island. At any rate, the secret is partly out, thanks to that unctuous idiot Guillot, and secrets being what they are, it's not going to rest until it escapes its prison."

"And you think I might be able to help you solve it?"

"Yes I do."

She laughed. "By mans of poetic intuition?"

"No—by taking it to someone who might have the necessary expertise, to whom you have access and I don't."

Hecate didn't need that spelling out—not simply because of her intelligence, but because she was feeling twinges of conscience.

"It's not what you think," she said. "I was going to tell you about it. You know I don't have any secrets from you...not for long, anyway. I just wanted to see whether I could do it first, so I didn't risk making a fool of myself."

Intelligent as I am, I couldn't make sense of that without further information. "You don't owe me an explanation, Hecate," I told her, mildly, "and you're perfectly entitled to keep as many secrets as you wish. It's really none of my business why you've been visiting the Convent, or even why the Mother Superior has been asking you questions about me. But if what you said yesterday about her having a better library than Niklaus Hylne, and being a genuine scholar, is true, then she probably has a better chance than he has of helping us figure out what this weird script might be."

Hecate nodded. "I'll take it to her," she agreed. She kept her eyes on the mysterious symbols, not because she was trying to understand them but because she didn't want to meet mine. "I'm probably too old to be learning new tricks, and after some of the things I've said in the past, I feel a bit of a hypocrite, but... thanks for understanding. Why did Vashti Savage ask you to go to see her yesterday?"

It really didn't seem fair that Hecate was asking for my explanations while stubbornly refusing to let go of hers, but I knew that she wasn't trying to cheat me. She really was embarrassed about whatever reason she had for visiting the Sisters of Shalimar, and needed a little more time to collect herself.

It could have been argued, too, that as Vashti had been so careful to conceal the favor she had asked of me from her companions in the Sprite, including Hecate, I owed her an obligation of confidentiality, but I'm a painter, not a physician or a notary.

"She's been having a recurrent dream," I told her. "Naturally, she construes it as a vision. She thought I might be able to help clarify it. I tried."

"A vision of what?" Hecate asked.

"Eurydice. She didn't know it was Eurydice, but she does now."

"Ah," said Hecate. It was more of a sigh than an exclamation of comprehension.

I waited; I knew there was more to come, on that subject as well as the matter of the Convent.

There was, of course, a third topic of interest suspended between us, and Hecate still needed time, even though she was now fully dressed.

"I've made friends with Mariette Parenot," she told me. "I like her. I promised that I'd go to see her tomorrow, when they've sorted things out. That shouldn't take long, as you've lent them Jean-Jacques and Luzon."

She paused, but that was merely the preface. She had something to tell me.

"And?" I prompted, obligingly.

"She's frightened. You probably noticed it in the Sprite."

"I did," I confirmed. "The little girl seemed uncertain too... except that in the mother, it's a straightforward anxiety, whereas in the child... well, perhaps it's simply because she is a child, and hasn't yet learned how to be frightened."

Hecate looked at me directly for the first time. "That's an odd thing to say, Axel. Does one have to learn how to be frightened?"

"Certainly," I said. "The thrill of the nerves might be reflexive, excited by stimuli external to consciousness, but conscious fear, the interpretation of fear, requires education and practice, just like every other conscious emotion."

"Including love?"

"Especially love."

She was looking at me hard now, but for the moment, she went back to Mariette's anxieties, "They didn't leave the Capital because Myrica talked them into coming to the island," Hecate told me. "If my guess is right, all three of them would rather have stayed where they were, and maintained their relationship as it was, in the safety of established habit, but... Vashti's not the only one afflicted by recurrent dreams, and not all of them are as ethereal as visions of Eurydice. Mariette has been troubled, and has become convinced that their house on Martyr's Mount was haunted. I don't know whether Parenot has felt anything directly, but in a household, one person's haunting automatically becomes everybody's. They felt they couldn't stay there. Except, of course… you know how these things work."

"Not really," I admitted, "but if what Niklaus said is true, I assume that what Mariette is really frightened of is that now Parenot no longer needs her too look after the child, he'll no longer need her, period—and she doesn't want not to be needed. And what the child would probably be frightened of, if she'd learned how, is what all sensitive children ought to be frightened of when they get to her age: growing up.

"I gather from Myrica that Parenot has a long struggle to arrive at the kind of financial security he's now acquired, not because he lacks ability but because his work is too conventional, too ordinary. He trained with Yvain Deloffre in the days when the great man used to take in pupils and was at the height of his arrogance, and Parenot is still painting the way Deloffre taught him to paint, still following Deloffre's rules and conventions, like a dozen other mythological painters I could name.

"While it was all a struggle, compounded by the responsibility of looking after the foundling, they were presumably a tightly-knit unit, just trying to get from one day to the next. Now… Elise is growing up, very evidently, even without praise being heaped on her supposed musical ability, Parenot has all kinds of possibilities in front of him, and Mariette must fear that she might become surplus to requirements. They've represented coming to the island to themselves as making a fresh start, but they're probably all anxious that it might actually be the end, the disintegration of what they had and a plunge into the abyss of the unknown."

"I told you that you know how these things work," Hecate said, with a wry smile. "Except that in this particular case, there's something else, something strange..."

"There always is," I said. "Generalizations only see the pattern, but every individual case is different. Eurydice is everywoman, but every woman is different. Mariette isn't your Eurydice—or Vashti's. As I said about Parenot's painting, although it's obvious that she's supposed to be a shade, there's nothing else distinctive about the image—she could be anyone. I thought of that, reflexively, as a flaw, but perhaps it isn't. Perhaps it's the whole point: Eurydice can be anyone to the contemplater of the image and the legend, and her lament can be anyone's lament. She's ubiquitous."

"It isn't just growing up that's frightening," Hecate observed, with a sigh. "That's just what's frightening at twelve. When you get to our age... it's growing old that frightens us." She wasn't thinking about herself, although she was keenly away of every hint of deterioration she saw in the mirror. She was thinking about Vashti Savage, and the possible significance of *her* visions of the potentially-ubiquitous Eurydice.

"It comes to us all," I said, simply because it was neutral, conventional and meaningless.

"Except you," said Hecate, with a hint of envy. "You don't look a day older than the day I met you."

"I've been fortunate," I admitted. "My deterioration has been mostly internal. If I really were the sorcerer that Constable Clovis and all the other superstitious fools on the island suspect me of being, though, I'd take twenty years off my appearance and manifest myself as a young Adonis."

Again, the comment was conventional and expectable, and that was why I had made it—but Hecate was still looking me in the eyes, and she knew me better than anyone else in the world.

"That's a lie," she said, with a slight hint of surprise at the realization. "Doubtless, if and when you were a young Adonis, you reveled in it—but it wouldn't suit your image now at all. Now, you're a great artist, and you can't project that image without a suitable maturity, an appropriate appearance of experience that implies wisdom and world-weariness. If you really were a sorcerer, and could paint your own portrait in your flesh, you'd be exactly what you are, and have been for... for as long as I've known you, and God only knows how much longer."

She was absolutely right of course, but it was only to be expected. I couldn't have loved her as much as I did if she hadn't had that intelligence and insight as well as her physical charms.

"Is Vashti's infatuation becoming problematic?" I asked her, by way of deflection. "I don't know what the precise significance is of the stirrings of her unconscious, but she's certainly wound up."

Hecate sighed again. "Yes," she said. "I thought that might be one of the advantages of getting older— that I wouldn't give rise to any more obsessions. And it seems to work, with the boys, although, as you know very well, that relief is mingled with regret. But with Vashti... it's a different matter. I'd have no problem with allowing her to make love to me, although it's not my preference, as you also know... but she wants far more than that. She wants *possession*. That I can't give her, and can't pretend—but there doesn't seem to be any way of curing her of the ambition. I have more sympathy with Mariette, if you're right about her fears, although, in the abstract, she could do without that level of commitment much more easily than Vashti. She's young, beautiful…but none of us has command over her heart, does she? At the end of the day, no one can command their emotions… except perhaps you."

"Not even me," I told her, and not because it was as the conventional, neutral, expectable thing to say. I was swift to add: "I hate to hurry you, but I really would like to get that puzzle to the Mother Superior as soon as possible. There seems to be something of a race developing, and you know how I hate to lose a race."

"I'll go right away," she said. "You must be in a hurry, if you're prepared to send me away before I've explained why I've been going to the Convent."

"As I said, you're perfectly entitled to keep secrets from me, for whatever reason you please," I assured her, knowing that she was at least going to tell me, even if she wasn't going to provide an elaborate explanation.

"I've changed my mind about musical accompaniment," she said, bluntly. "But I don't want to work with anyone else, so I'm learning to play an instrument myself—the marine trumpet."

She was already on her way out of the door, not so much hurrying to fulfill my commission by taking the cryptogram to the Mother Superior, but running away to hide her embarrassment.

I let her run.

VII. Clarifications

One puzzle, at least, had now been clarified. Hecate had not said much, but she had said enough for me to work out the rest. She was a lyric poet living in an artists' colony replete with ambitious musicians, many of them as ambitious in the business of seduction as they were in their art—and many of whom made no little or no distinction between music and seduction, considering the playing of their instruments as an intrinsically amorous exercise. Players of stringed instruments, in particular, expert in fingering the strings and wielding the bow, tended to be keenly aware of the potential symbolism of their actions and the potential effects of their harmonic productions. Nor was there any misrepresentation in that awareness, because music really does have the power to stir the emotions, to simulate and to stimulate amour.

Hecate was a beautiful woman. Some men, in fact, might consider her even more beautiful now, in her maturity, than she had been in the full bloom of her youth. Tastes differ, and change. In my youth—when I was, I fear, by no means an Adonis—I had yearned and pined after young women, who had set the standard of beauty for me. Now, although I could still appreciate the beauty of youth, and still pay homage to it in my art, I could also appreciate a broader spectrum of beauty, with more subtle hints and hues, and I was a better artist for it, because it increased my sensitivity. Hence, I appreciated Hecate no less now than in her younger days, and perhaps even more.

In her younger days, however, the tendency of young men to become infatuated with her and obsessed by her had been more marked, and by virtue of her environment, the laws of probability had dictated that a high percentage of them were musicians, who did everything possible to use their own artistry as temptation. One such stratagem, obviously, had been that of aspiring to accompany her lyric poetry with their instruments, to fuse their art with hers in a representation of the carnal fusion they desired.

Abundantly possessed of carnal desires of her own, Hecate had never been unafraid to indulge them, with musicians as with others, but she had been no more willing then than she was now to grant anyone *possession* of her body, her soul, or—above all—her art. She had known full well for a long time, aided by a few bitter experiences, that she did not have sufficient command over her emotions to sustain her particular lusts for very long. Like me, she was incapable of sustaining the kind of ideal of love that Vashti Savage and many other people tried to maintain: the notion that one single individual could supply all of a person's emotional and existential needs permanently. Like me, she considered that notion of "true" love to be essentially illusory, and the obsessive determination many people seem to have to find or achieve to be rooted in psychological anxiety rather than reality.

For that reason, although she had surrendered her flesh to musicians when the whim took her, she had *never* allowed them to become her accompanist in what she considered to be the more precious and intimate sense, by allowing them to fuse their music with her poetry, and their creative process with hers. She had always justified that refusal by means of an esthetic argument, insisting that her poetry, although lyric in a technical sense, was wrought for the voice alone, and could not be ameliorated by any musical accompaniment.

Ill-wishers, of course—and even Hecate had a few, beauty having its costs as well as its benefits—had always suggested that her insistence was simply a consequence of her inability to play a musical instrument, and her incompetence in fully understanding the potential of music. It was an argument I had heard voiced several times, sometimes by jealous women and sometimes by discarded lovers. False or not, it had inevitably become something of a sore point, relative to which even I could not have a safe discussion with Hecate.

Now, apparently she had changed her mind, or at least retreated slightly from the position she had defended so assertively for so many years. She had decided that her latest work, "Eurydice's Lament," would benefit from musical accompaniment, and therefore needed musical accompaniment, which she was determined to provide herself. I had no doubt that she had come to that conclusion on purely artistic grounds, and that her choice of an instrument was made on the same grounds, and not because she thought that a marine trumpet might be the easiest instrument to learn, by virtue of only having one string—an assumption which would, I assumed, have been false, although I could not claim to be an expert.

A marine trumpet is not a kind of trumpet. It is, in fact, a single-stringed instrument from which a range of sounds can be extracted by various manipulations of the single string, adapting its length by applying pressure at various points along an extent considerably greater than the typical length of the strings of multi-stringed instruments. Effectively, one can imagine a marine trumpet as a kind of viol—perhaps more akin to a cello than a violin—which has its strings mounted sequentially rather than in parallel.

Most marine trumpets are as tall as a man, or even taller, but they are, for historical reasons, almost exclusively played by women. The evolution of musical instruments through the ages has a somewhat checkered history, entangled with the history of prostitution as well as the history of religion—which two contexts have not always separated themselves fully—but in the case of the marine trumpet the evolution mostly took place in a religious context, beginning with the rites of the mystery religions and continuing in the tradition of monachism that developed in such exoteric religions as Christianity and Druidism—both of which, of course, laid claim to the invention and accused the other of imitation.

Whatever the truth of the matter—and it has been severely confused as well as concealed by deliberate mystery—there was a period in the history of the Empire's various religions when it was considered indecent for women to play the trumpet, presumably because the operations of the mouth and effects on the cheeks were uncomfortably reminiscent of operations not involving cold brass. As a result of that, trumpets and similar instruments were restricted in various religious ceremonies to male performers, while females were restricted to stringed instruments, perhaps primarily and at least including the one that was called a marine trumpet, not because it had anything to do with the sea, but because of feminine associations with the name Marie, itself connected with the etymology of words such as "maternity."

At any rate, to cut a long and inescapably vague story short, the only marine trumpets on Mnemosyne, and the only habitual players of the marine trumpet, in the present Age of Not-Quite-Enlightenment, were to be found in the Convent of the Sisters of Shalimar, where the distaff side of the ancient bardic tradition was supposedly maintained as a kind of devotion. Hence, Hecate Rain's regular visits to the Convent: she was, as she had baldly declared, without further explanation, learning to play the marine trumpet.

Evidently, she was taking lessons from the Mother Superior herself. Equally evidently, the Sisters were willing to let her take one of their instruments out of the Convent, when the time came, so that she could accompany herself when she gave public performances of "Eurydice's Lament," which she was presumably planning to do when the tourist season began again in late spring.

Perhaps, given that I now knew that the Mother Superior was not bound to seclusion, the entire company of Sisters of Shalimar would be in the audience, kindly overlooking the blatant paganism of the poem's theme in the spirit of religious tolerance that the successors of the Divine Julius had been wise enough to make into one of the cardinal principles of Imperial organization. History might have been very different if the Divine Julius had been as jealous as certain other gods I could name—for one thing, the Empire might have been smashed to smithereens by religious wars and schisms, as had become a very real threat more than once.

Was it, I wondered about to become a threat again? Surely not, if what was coming to the surface in the matter of Monsieur de Toustain's enigmatic legacy was a squabble between the rival cults of Orpheus and Dionysus. No matter how successful the residues of the cults were in matters of political promotion, they were still small-scale affairs, deliberately exclusive and esoteric. They could not possibly threaten the kinds of upheavals that had occasionally been threatened by exoteric creeds that boasted millions of adherents, such as Christianity and its eternal rival, Druidism. The battle of the saints against the bards really had been on the brink of eruption into civil war more than once in the last two thousand years—but the Empire's essentially secular military organization had always quelled the storm, enforcing compulsory tolerance, in spite of the paradoxicality of the oxymoron, just as it had always withstood so-called barbarian invasions from without.

And the Empire had, in my view, always been right, even if its methods had occasionally been a trifle brutal. It really was in the interests of adherents of all religions to live in peace rather than seeking to exterminate one another, and it really was in the interests of barbarians to learn the disciple of civilization. Whether the ends justified the means or not, they were ends worth fighting for, and worthy of attainment. Where would arts like mine be, if the Empire had dissolved into chaos? I couldn't think about it without shuddering. And if one looked at it cynically—as I, inevitably, tended to do—didn't religions thrive on martyrs? Didn't they benefit from memories of oppression and the heroes who had been prepared to die for the faith? Weren't the Christians proud of having a Martyr's Mount in the Capital, even if it was nowadays the abode of artists, whores and apaches? One cannot truly appreciate the value and benefits of peace without having experienced the occasional lack of it—and that applies on the personal level as well as the provincial and imperial levels. All in all, it is not entirely a bad thing that peace of mind is sometimes difficult to obtain, and that the emotions we cannot command sometimes pose inordinately stern challenges to its attainment.

Such were the ideas that were running through my mind while I walked home, hunching my shoulders against the unseasonable chill, and groping with my lungs for a satisfaction that was somehow no longer fully present in the air. I had grown used to the slightly strange odor, but it was still there; there really was something wrong with the atmosphere, and it really was ominous, if only in a purely physical and natural sense. I suddenly had an impression of how tiny and vulnerable humans are in the face of elements that are far beyond their control. Do we really need the supernatural, when a trivial change in the behavior of the sun, or the arrival of some unexpected comet from the depths of space, could bring civilization on the surface of our insignificant globe to an abrupt end?

I tried to shove those ideas to the back of my mind and concentrate on something more comfortable as well as more authentically urgent. I thought that I might perhaps be able to get a little work done, in spite of the poor light, now that I had delegated the mystery of the Toustain legacy to hopefully-competent authorities.

It was, of course, an optimistic chimera. I was caught up in something now, and whatever it was, its toils were not going to let me go without a struggle.

There was a carriage waiting outside my house when I arrived, and inside the carriage, less than happy about having had to wait on the road, was the Marquis de Mesmay.

"I rang," he said, stonily, "but there was no answer."

"My profuse apologies, Milord," I said. "I sent my servants to help a new neighbor move in." I waved a hand vaguely in the direction of the former Toustain house.

I opened the door myself and showed the Marquis directly into the studio, partly because I assumed that he had come to see how his triptych was coming along, and partly because there was still no fire in the drawing room. I busied myself stoking up the one in the studio while my client scrutinized the middle panel of the project, doubtless measuring the progress I had made since the last time he had called.

"I'm truly sorry to have forced you to wait outside, Milord," I said, when I had finished. "At least we can be glad that the north-west wind has not resumed yesterday's force, and the snow did not settle, even if it has left the roads a little muddier than usual."

I expected him to tell me that he hadn't come to talk to me about the weather, but apparently it was not a topic of complete disinterest to him.

"Did you notice anything anomalous about that snow, Master Rathenius?" he asked.

"Yes I did," I admitted. "It appeared to be impregnated with soot."

"That's what you think it was?"

"I don't know," I admitted. "I can't think of any other explanation."

"The soot is accountable," he said, as if he were agreeing with me, "but how do you account for the pillar of fire that is supposed to have produced it?"

He had me completely at a loss. I could only repeat: "Pillar of fire?"

"You haven't been down to the harbor, then?"

"No, Milord, I've been visiting friends."

"You must have walked back briskly, to stay ahead of the rumor. The crews of two boats that docked this morning, having been fishing in the Oceanic waters beyond the Breton Isles, reported that a gigantic pillar of fire had been seen rising out of the Ocean the night before last."

I took note of the formulation of the report: the pillar *had been seen*; the crews of the boats had not claimed to have seen it themselves. They were passing on second hand rumor, gleaned at sea or in the ports of the Breton Isles. Under other circumstances, I might have assumed that it was a tall tale or a hallucination—but I had seen the black snow.

On the other hand, a pillar of fire emerging from the Atlantic! That merely pushed the prodigy one step back, without making it any less prodigious. Quite the contrary in fact.

"The fishermen are saying that it's an omen," Mesmay added. "The islanders are a superstitious lot, I know, who see omens everywhere, but still... if gigantic pillars of fire can't qualify as omens, what can?"

"Indeed, Milord," I said, nodding my head.

"By nightfall," the Marquis continued "they'll doubtless have come up with some ancient prophecy, Bardic or Christian, real or invented, making the prodigy a sign of some kind... perhaps of the end of the world..."

He was evidently fishing, but for what, and why? His speculations were closely akin to my own, and naturally so, but that only made me want to try even harder to defuse them.

"I've never heard any mention of pillars of fire in all the years I've been on the island," I told him, "and I must have heard all the local legends by now. If there's any ready-made implication in the stories the fishermen are telling, I have no idea what it is."

He nodded, as if any agreement or sympathy. "And how many years have you been on the island, Master Rathenius?" he asked, too casually for the question to be genuinely casual, even if it hadn't been a question that suddenly seemed to be on everybody's mind.

Given that at least one person was supposed to be able to put a number on it, and there really were hundreds of indigenes old enough to remember a time when I hadn't been here, I saw no reason not to tell the truth.

"Twenty-seven years," I said.

"That's time enough to get to know it thoroughly," he observed, as if conceding a point. "Tell me, Master Rathenius, do you know whether the Cult of Dionysus has any presence on the island?"

I wasn't taken by surprise by that. I answered, with all evident frankness: "Not so far as I'm aware—but as it's supposed to be a secret society, I assume that if it did have any presence here, it would have done everything possible to prevent my being aware of it, just as the Cult of Orpheus would have done, with exactly the same result. Can I offer you something to drink, by the way, Milord? Do sit down, if you've finished studying the painting."

The double deflection seemed to work. He did take a seat, in the armchair I'd brought up to the fire for Tommaso Dellacrusca, and he did accept a glass of wine—but when I sat down with him, he got back to the point.

"I assume that you're mentioning the Cult of Orpheus because you've heard rumor that I might be a member of it?"

"I've even heard rumor that I might be a member of it, or of its mortal rival," I confirmed. "People who are accustomed to look for omens and hidden meanings in everything easily draw the wrong inference from appearances. You've commissioned me to produce a triptych of paintings on the subject of the Orpheus myth. That's enough, in the minds of some superstitious people, who already suspect me of being a magician, to imply probable membership in a secret cult. We both know how ridiculous that is, because we both know that an artistic appreciation of the symbolism of mythology is a world away from any kind of religious belief or political conspiracy."

"Indeed," said Mesmay. "I understand, by the way, that your new neighbor is the painter whose *Eurydice* I have hanging in my a small drawing room?"

"He is," I said. "And he has brought his Eurydice with him. She's as beautiful in the flesh as she is in the painting, although necessarily a trifle less ethereal."

"Of course," he agreed. "I could see when Madame Mavor first showed me the painting that it had been painted with love. He paints her often, I understand, in various roles—but only Eurydice would allow him to imagine himself as Orpheus. I said as much to Madame Mavor, and she told me that he is indeed a music lover, a skilled performer on the violin."

"So I believe."

"And he has a prodigy of his own, if what Madame Mavor says is true—a daughter with a genuine gift. Since she's here, and there's so little to do in the dead season, we really ought to make arrangements to hear her, don't you think?"

"She's very young," I said, "and with all due respect to Myrica, she does have a tendency to exaggerate, only natural in an artists' agent. I met the girl last night, and she seemed to me to be rather shy. I'm not sure that she's ready yet to give concerts."

"Still," said the Marquis, with more insistence than I thought the situation warranted, "we must make our new guests welcome—and Parenot is one of the artists whose work I've patronized. I really ought to organize a reception for him at my house, so that he can be properly introduced to Fion Commonal and the other members of the Island Council, and other notables... all the more so as Madame Mavor's hastily-improvised reception seems to have been a disappointment to all concerned."

I took note of his use of the phrase *our new guests*, suggesting that he was indeed beginning to think of himself as a resident of the island and not merely a summer visitor.

"That's a kind thought, Milord," I said trying not to sound too unenthusiastic, and wondering what his hidden agenda might be.

"And it would be a perfect opportunity for the young prodigy to make her debut, don't you think?"

"Perhaps," I said, no longer attempting to dissimulate my lack of enthusiasm, "but as I said, Milord, I really don't think that she's ready to play in public, and it wouldn't be kind to invite her to do it. She's very young."

"We shall see," he said, serenely. "It's very kind of you to have lent them your servants to help them settle into the old Toustain house. I imagine that it will require a good deal of work to render it comfortable."

"I don't know," I said. "I've never been inside."

"Really? I understood that you and Toustain were friends?"

"Nodding acquaintances," I said, by way of polite correction. "As a painter, who spends a great deal of time absorbed in my work, I prefer not to have much interaction with my neighbors. Monsieur de Toustain seemed to feel the same way."

I expected him to bring up the legacy then, but he didn't—not directly, at least.

"But you know, don't you, that Toustain was not his real name?"

"I hadn't the slightest idea of it until last night. Apparently, there's a rumor going round to that effect, but I don't know whether to believe it. The island's rumors are not renowned for their reliability." I was tempted to add: *People even claim to have seen pillars of fire rising out of the sea*, as an example of their unreliability, but I didn't. I had held its soot in the palm of my hand.

"You can believe it," Mesmay assured me. "I have it from his notary, who is now mine."

I knew that it was a risky move, but I didn't want to leave all the fishing to him. "And is that why you asked me about the Cult of Dionysus?" I said.

"Yes it is," he said. "But you were only nodding acquaintances, you say? So you would never have had any reason to suspect him of being a Dionysian, whatever meaning one can attach to the term nowadays?"

He still hadn't mentioned the legacy, but the absence was beginning to become conspicuous, and provocative.

"No reason at all," I said. "At least until I found the parchment hidden in the binding of one of the books he left me." There was no point in keeping quiet about it: the whole point of giving a copy to Niklaus Hylne had been to spread the news, so that any gangs of Italian bravos who happened to land on the island would discover that their cat was out of the bag.

"A parchment?" Mesmay repeated, in a voice whose intonation was almost as indecipherable as the mysterious symbols.

"Yes," I said. "Would you like to see it? I can't make head nor tail of it, so I've sent copies to various scholars here and in the Capital, in the hope that one of them can unravel its meaning."

Mesmay was keeping his face rigidly straight, but he looked a good deal paler now than when he had sat down, in spite of the fact that I had stoked up the fire. He was trying hard to conceal an intense interest, and the strain was showing.

"You've sent copies...," he echoed, as if he were having difficulty believing it.

"Yes," I said. "I have no way of knowing, of course, whether it has any connection with the Cult of Dionysus, and I don't suppose any of the scholars will be able to work it out, either, but I thought that I ought to make an effort, in the interests of scholarship."

"Of course," he said. It wasn't the feeblest *of course* I'd ever heard, but it was a close-run contest. He didn't take long to add: "May I see the parchment?"

I went to fetch it from the hiding-place in the wine-cellar in which I'd placed it, and set it down on a table in the studio. "It's rather fragile, I'm afraid," I told him. "It's perhaps best if we don't handle to too much."

He didn't object. Indeed, there seemed to be a certain reverence in the way that he bent down to inspect the parchment, scanning it very carefully with a gaze that seemed extremely intense.

That contemplation lasted for several minutes— almost as if he were trying to commit the image to memory, or striving to find an intuition that would permit him to grasp its meaning.

"Do you know what script it's written in" I hazarded.

"No," was the inevitable reply. I had no idea whether the denial was honest or not, but I felt sure that he knew something—or, to be strictly accurate, that he *thought* he knew something—that he wasn't about to share with me.

I still didn't have the faintest idea what was going on, but I was certain, now, that something was, and that it was something bigger and broader than I'd initially been able to suspect. There were far too many coincidences for there not to be a hidden pattern, and somehow, somewhere at the heart of that pattern, was Orpheus… or Eurydice.

Mesmay, when his contemplation of the parchment was finally concluded, didn't return to the armchair by the fire. Instead, he went back to the unfinished triptych. This time, however, he wasn't studying the middle panel, to which I was slowly applying paint. He was looking at the third panel, which was only a charcoal sketch as yet: the image of the severed head of Orpheus, floating downriver, still singing, and still charming, issuing its own lament for the terrible fate of his hopes, his dreams and his music.

He studied it for as long as he had studied the parchment, and then he turned back to me.

"What happened to him, in the version of the myth you had in mind when you sketched it?"

"He was murdered by maenads," I answered, although I knew that wasn't what he meant.

"Yes," he said, "but why?"

He actually wanted an answer. He thought that in order to paint the picture, in order to exert the full force of my artistry, I needed to insert myself into the myth, to intuit the hidden rationale behind its symbolism. And he wasn't entirely wrong—but I couldn't give him the kind of neat clarification for which he was asking. Not yet, at any rate.

"The conventional explanation," I said, "which is said to be the opinion of the Orphic cult, is that Dionysus ordered the maenads to kill him, because of some real or imagined betrayal. Dionysus is said to have regarded him as a pupil or protégé who had overstepped his bounds—but I've never believed that. In my conception of the myth, which I'm trying to incarnate in the triptych, Dionysus has nothing to do with it. The maenads weren't acting on his orders—if, indeed, they were maenads that killed him, rather than someone who merely put the blame on maenads in order to implicate the followers of Dionysus."

"Why, then, was he murdered?" Mesmay persisted.

I had no alternative but honesty. "I don't know," I said. "Not yet—and perhaps I'll never figure it out, although something might well occur to me, as it often does while a work of art is in progress. I hope it will—but whether it does or not, I'll finish the painting, and you won't have any reason to find fault with it. Some things benefit from remaining mysterious and insoluble, and some things just are, whether we like it or not. Art is as much a matter of working around uncertainty as it is of penetrating it."

Mesmay was no fool. He understood what I was saying, and he believed me, as he had every reason to do.

"The other explanation that is sometimes offered in the literature," he said, speculatively, "is that the maenads were avenging Eurydice—that they blamed him for his failure to be reunited with her, either because he was too cowardly to rejoin her by dying himself, or because he didn't follow through with his effort to bring her out of the Underworld."

"I'm familiar with the hypothesis," I confirmed.

"But you don't believe that one either?"

"I'm not sure that it's completely wrong, but no—in the way that you've just phrased the two alternatives, I don't believe either of them. I'm still looking for something else, just as...," I stopped, fearing a breach of confidentiality—but there was no need; he knew what I meant.

"Just as your friend Hecate Rain is searching, in composing her poem," Mesmay completed for me.

"Yes," I admitted.

Then he said something rather remarkable: "Do you think she might be able to finish it in time to perform it, when I host a reception for Charles Parenot and his Eurydice?"

I hesitated, but told the truth. "I doubt it," I said. "From what I've seen, it still needs a lot of work, and Hecate doesn't like to hurry her work. I don't think she's planning on any kind of public reading before the spring, when the season starts again."

Mesmay nodded his head. "Well," he said, "we can hope. Sometimes, inspiration hurries things along."

It seemed that he wanted to hurry a lot of things along. I wondered exactly what kind of reception he had in mind.

"I'll work on the paintings as hard as I can," I assured him. "Sometimes, as you say, inspiration permits an acceleration—but sometimes, it takes its time. I'm sure you want my best work, not my fastest."

"I do," he said. "And I leave the matter entirely in your hands. I trust your artistry... your genius. When the time comes, I'm sure that you'll understand what happened to Orpheus, and that your understanding will work wonders."

By this time, I was fully convinced that he really was a member of the Cult of Orpheus, and not merely in the sense that he was part of some secret cabal of plotters hoping to gain political control of the provincial capital. He too was searching for something beyond the conventional, and the reason that he had commissioned me to paint the triptych was because he thought I might be able to help him, without even being aware of it...and not only me. I even wondered, crazy as it seemed, whether he had hung the picture of Eurydice in his small drawing room in order that Vashti Savage might see it while trying to channel his wife's dead mother.

"I'll do my very best," I assured him.

"As always," he said. "Madame Mavor has convinced me of that. She exaggerates, as you say, but she's very knowledgeable, and when she tells me that you're a veritable sorcerer, who can work wonders, I believe her. I believe in you, Master Rathenius."

It was, I suppose very kind of him, and a true testament to my genius. I only hoped—and it was a hope that I had rarely entertained before—that he wasn't overestimating me.

VIII. Historical Expertise

By the time the Marquis de Mesmay had gone, my head was so full of potential raw material for meditation that I needed distraction and absorption, so I ate a hasty lunch, prepared by my own hands, and returned to the studio to take up my paints for a while. I was also feeling a trifle guilty at the slowness of my endeavor, to which the Marquis had made every attempt to apply a spur. I launched myself into work on the middle panel, on the host of shades charmed by Orpheus, visible only from behind as a silhouette, although a part of his lyre could be glimpsed and his stance left no doubt that he was playing.

The absorption worked, and I was soon in a near trance, losing track of time completely once I had lit a lamp to assist the dim gray daylight that seemed to be crawling rather than flooding through the windows. When the doorbell rang I naturally ignored it, and it was not until it rang for a second time that it occurred to me that there was no one to answer it, because Jean-Jacques was still at the old Toustain house.

I cursed, and blinked, and realized, too, that the light had become positively sepulchral, perhaps more suited to the painting of an Underworld scene than bright and cheerful sunlight, but so gloomy nevertheless that it was not providing adequate assistance to my vision, even with the aid of the lamp. Night had not yet fallen, though; behind the masses of gray cloud, the sun was still above the horizon.

It was snowing again, and this time, the snow was swirling in a capricious wind.

When the doorbell rang for the third time, I could not ignore it any longer. Cursing even more volubly, I went to open the door.

It was a woman I had never seen before, short and a trifle stout, although it was difficult to estimate her age because her features were partly hidden by the voluminous hood of a black cloak, which she had pulled up to protect her from the wind and snow. Because the garment was black, it was impossible to tell at a glimpse whether or not the snow was still polluted by soot from the alleged pillar of fire jetting from the Ocean.

"Please tell your Master that Sister Ursule wishes to see him—Sister Ursule from the Covent of Shalimar," the visitor said, not really looking at me because she was hunching her shoulders and bowing her head to shield herself from the elements, but obviously assuming that I was a servant.

There was no carriage in the road. The sister had evidently walked. I hastened to usher her inside and took her into the studio, sitting her down in the chair by the fire and stoking it up yet again before even introducing myself.

"I'm truly sorry for making you wait, Sister," I said. "It had slipped my mind that my manservant is not here to answer the door, so I did not respond immediately."

"There's no need to apologize," the sister replied, pushing back her hood to reveal the cream head-dress of the Sisters of Shalimar. I hastened to take her cloak, and found the remainder of the costume underneath, unstained by the snow because of the protective cloak, which I carefully hung on a peg in the hallways before returning to my unexpected visitor. A few wisps of silvery hair were protruding from the severe head-dress, and a slightly wizened face that must have been regally handsome a long time ago, revealed her age; they gave their owner a commanding presence in spite of her short stature: antiquity and desiccation had weathered the features into a quiet but firm authority.

While she was realizing that I was, in fact, Axel Rathenius, I realized in my turn that she was not simply a sister bringing me a message from the Mother Superior of the convent, but the Mother Superior herself.

We looked at one another for a few more seconds, in rapid appraisal, and then her gaze strayed, to take in the studio, and all its clutter. I could see how she had impressed Hecate and convinced her that she possessed a wisdom beyond the usual. I sensed that her glance really was taking the measure of me, as an artist rather than merely a person who could not quite keep his art in order.

All I could think of to say was: "You really shouldn't have walked all the way out to the headland in weather like this, Sister Ursule."

"I walk everywhere," she said. "I've been up Snowspur in worse. I'm getting old, but I'm not helpless."

I sat down in the other chair, not yet fully recovered from the broken concentration, and still not knowing what to say. Somehow, even though I'd been told that she sometimes went out, the fact that the Mother Superior of the Convent had come to call on me seemed more prodigious than any mere blizzard of black snow or pillar of fire.

"I felt that I ought to come in person," she said, once she had realized that I wasn't going to say anything more for the moment. "And I confess, in fact, that I was curious to meet you. One way and another, I've heard a great deal about you."

"From poor Eirene," I said, "and Hecate Rain."

"Mostly," she agreed.

Who else, then? I wondered.

"You have me at a disadvantage, I'm afraid," I said, as my mind finally clicked into gear, like a well-oiled press. "I've hardly heard a single word about you, in more than twenty years, from Eirene Magdelana, Hecate or anyone else. I can't even console myself with the thought that what you've heard about me might be misleading, for no one knows me better than Hecate... although no one could see quite as far into my soul as Eirene."

"Their accounts did seem more reliable than others I've heard," she said, without naming the others in question. "I fear, Master Rathenius, that I've come to bring you a warning: the parchment you've discovered is something that certain people might be prepared to kill to obtain. I understand that you've made other copies than the one you sent to me. Do you mind my asking who has seen them?"

"I sent one to the Capital," I told her, "and gave another to Niklaus Hylne—and the Marquis of Mesmay has seen the original. I was alone with him at the time, but he didn't make any attempt to kill me." I was trying to lighten the tone, but I wasn't entirely sure that it warranted lightening.

"Oh, Antoine won't try to kill you," she said. "In fact, it might be as well that he's seen it—he might be able to defend you more effectively than you could yourself."

The most surprising thing about that remark was her use of what I assumed to be the Marquis of Mesmay's first name. I had never heard anyone refer to him in any other way than by his surname or title. I had assumed that his first name was only employed by his wife, and probably only in the privacy of their bedroom.

"Who might try to kill me to take possession of it, then?" I asked.

"If my understanding to the situation is correct, the Dionysians," she replied, forthrightly.

"You can read it, then?" I queried.

"I can't read it," she replied, "but I believe that I know what it is—or, to be strictly accurate, what the late Monsieur de Toustain believed it to be."

Naturally, she stopped there. She was not without a sense of theater. She was, after all, consciously acting out a melodrama of her own, and seemingly taking some pleasure in it.

She stood up, and walked over to the table. It was only then that I realized that I had not taken the parchment back to the wine-cellar after showing it to Mesmay. If anyone had turned up who was intent on stealing it, they would not have had to go to a great deal of trouble to find it, once they had shot me.

Sister Ursule peered at the parchment as intensely as Mesmay had done, for what must have been almost exactly the same lapse of time.

"Interesting," was her verdict. "How did you send the copy to the Capital?"

"Discreetly," I said, and left it at that.

She nodded her head, apparently willing to take my word for it. "It was probably a wise move," she said. "The parchment itself is a copy, of course, albeit an old one; the original, if there ever was one, was destroyed a long time ago. Your copies are very artful, and you might well have disseminated them too widely for any-one to think it practicable to seize and destroy them all without attracting far too much unwelcome attention. Did you do that deliberately?"

"Yes," I said.

"So you knew that there was danger—and yet you gave a copy to Hecate?" She might have added "to give to me," but she didn't.

"I didn't have any other way of getting the document to you," I said, "and I thought, given what Hecate had told me about your library and knowledge of the myth of Orpheus, that you were probably the one person on the island who might be able to cast light on the matter. I didn't think that you'd be in danger. If the Dionysians, or anyone else with an interest in acquiring the parchment, don't want to attract attention, they're hardly likely to invade the Convent of the Sisters of Shalimar and murder the Mother Superior."

"It had occurred to me," she said, "that that might have been your principal reason for sending it to me."

I shook my head. "Hecate really did speak highly of your scholarly credentials," I said. "Evidently, she wasn't wrong. Will Niklaus Hylne be able to discover what the document is, do you think?"

Sister Ursule pursed her lips slightly. "I doubt it," she said. "The legend is sufficiently well documented, but in order to connect the document with the legend, he would have to be able to recognize the symbols in which it's inscribed. That's a more esoteric matter."

"And what are the symbols?" I asked. "Or is that a secret between you and the esoteric Bardic scriptures?"

She came back to the armchair and sat down. "Of course it's a secret," she said. "Somewhat less so now, thanks to you... or Monsieur de Toustain. But the legend, as I say, is documented, accessible to any dedicated antiquarian. If Monsieur Hylne is clever enough, or sufficiently inspired, he might be able to guess that the symbols are a fragment of the suspiric language."

"The language of sighs?" I queried.

"You've heard of it?"

"No—but I have some Latin."

"Of course. And you're acquainted with Madame Savage, are you not?"

"Yes," I admitted. "But I don't believe she's ever mentioned the language of sighs to me."

"It's one of the arcana of her discipline; she probably wouldn't have mentioned it to you even if she didn't think of you as an unsympathetic skeptic."

Hecate had obviously told her more about me, and other things, than she had implied. "I'm not quite following this," I said. "To be best of my knowledge, Shalimar was a visionary Bard, and your Order is a Druidic one. Vashti Savage is a spiritist medium. I thought they were two very different faiths."

"There is a philosophy that holds that there are no different faiths, but that all are one, cloaked in various symbolic languages—but in any case, spiritism is a method rather than a faith; it's not incompatible with any religion, including Druidism and Christianity, although neither faith really approves of it. On the other hand, the mystery religions are quite hospitable to necromancy of all kinds, perfectly willing to employ it on occasion."

Another piece of the puzzle clicked into place. The Marquise de Mesmay was a spiritist, but that apparently didn't mean that she couldn't be a member of the Cult of Orpheus too—or, at least, married to one." But it still didn't explain how the Mother Superior of the Sisters of Shalimar knew the Marquise de Mesmay—although, admittedly, she seemed to know a great many things that one wouldn't have expected her to know.

The simplest way is sometimes the best. "Do you know the Marquis de Mesmay well?" I asked, bluntly.

"I've never met him," she replied, equally bluntly, but added: "I don't really have much opportunity to enjoy the company of men; this is a rare privilege for me—but to answer the question more fully, I do know a good deal more about Antoine than most men, because he's married to my niece."

I must have looked more surprised than the revelation warranted, because she continued: "Even Sisters of Shalimar have actual sisters. Mine was Aethne's mother. Aethne and I aren't close nowadays, but we are still in touch. She used to seek my counsel quite often; it's less frequent now, but communication hasn't entirely ceased."

"Giving the Sisters of Shalimar a line of communication to the heart of the Orphean cult," I said.

"Not its heart, Master Rathenius, or even its wing... but a part of it, yes."

"Do you have other nieces married to Dionysians?"

"Alas, no... which might, I admit, give me slightly distorted view of that rival cult, most of whose members are probably meek clubmen. Still, just as there seem to be some Orpheans who regard the Dionysians as the direct descendants of the murderer of their founder, so there are rumored to be some Dionysians who regard the Orpheans as the treacherous slanderers of theirs. It probably seems as absurd to you as it does to me that a vendetta occasioned by an imaginary crime could extend over more than three thousand years, still drawing blood, but there have been political complications and schisms, as I suppose you're vaguely aware, which have served to keep hatred alive and occasionally to stoke it up. Even if that document is utterly meaningless, as it might well be, the mere fact of its existence and its history has been enough to cause murders in the past, and might continue to do so in future."

"Would you care to tell me why? Given that I'm currently holding the object of desire in question, albeit reluctantly, I'd like to know why someone might be prepared to kill me to take it from me—if, in fact, your judgment in that matter is correct."

"You're probably correct to doubt it—I'm uncomfortably aware myself that my knowledge of the world is limited to what I can obtain from books and the fragile lines of communication opened to me by a few confidantes. I might be completely mistaken—but I'll tell you what I know... except that some of it, I fear, is mere conjecture. No one really knows the truth, because no one really knows how to decode the myth of Orpheus' excursion to the Underworld.

"The legend pertaining to the manuscript of which your parchment is a partial copy claims that that when Orpheus succeeded in charming the shades with his music—including Hades and Persephone themselves—he was able to do it because he was inspired with the ability to play or sing the language of sighs: the language of the dead, which only Hades and the infernal judges were supposed to know how to write. Having learned to sing it, though, when Orpheus came out of the Underworld again, he contrived to write down the song he had sung: the song that has the gift not merely of charming shades, but of charming Hades, the god of death, himself. Whether he supposedly wrote it in Hades' own script, or whether he invented his own notation, is unclear, as is the precise content of what he wrote, which is probably more akin to a sequence of musical notes than words.

"Whatever the truth of the matter, Orpheus' alleged record of the charming of the dead, and of death itself, became one of the most precious artifacts of the ancient Orphean cult, guarded with the utmost jealousy, even though no one, after his death knew how to read it. The Orpheans believed that if and when the time came for it to be read and sung, the spirit of Orpheus would possess or inspire the destined player, and Orpheus' quest to liberate and reclaim Eurydice would be reenacted—successfully, this time.

"Before the appointed time arrived, however, in the course of one of the conflicts between the Orpheans and the Dionysians, the original document was destroyed. The Dionysians thought that that would put an end to the Orphean cult, or at least what the members of the cult regarded as their sacred quest, forever. However, the Orpheans believed, or at least put the word around, that several copies of the original document had been made, and that they were still being preciously guarded, all the more carefully because the original was gone. It's said that the Dionysians tried to hunt them down, and found one or two pieces of parchment that they burned religiously—but they could never be sure that what they'd destroyed were the actual copies, or whether or not they had destroyed them all. The rumor persisted for a very long time, as one might expect, that one copy was still out there, somewhere.

"Eventually, the Dionysians began to claim that they had found the last copy, but that, instead of destroying it, they were preserving it themselves, preciously, in order that when appointed time came, it would be one of their members, inspired by Dionysius, rather than one of their rivals, inspired by Orpheus, who would be able to charm death, and thus claim Eurydice and all that she represented, for themselves.

"The likelihood is that the assertion in question just a provocation: a kind of challenge, turning the tables on behalf of the cult that refused to die. In my personal opinion, what you have there is a forgery, of the same ilk as thousands of other supposedly sacred or magical documents, grimoires and the like—but I might be wrong. Even if it is a fake, though, and perhaps a fake of something that never had any real existence in the first place, it retains a certain symbolic value. If the Dionysians think that they had it, but that they've just lost it, and the Orpheans think that they've reclaimed it... well, even if it's a worthless piece of gibberish, it might have too much talismanic importance for the Dionysians not to want it back... and to want all the copies you've made destroyed."

I weighed all of that up, as carefully as I could. It was a farrago of nonsense, and I was inclined to agree with Sister Ursule that the parchment had to be a fake, of no real value—but the kind of fake that could nevertheless become a powerful desideratum.

"In effect," I said, "I've been caught in the middle of a feud between two gangs of lunatics. But why on earth would Toustain bequeath the poisoned chalice to me? Why not to one of his Dionysian friends?"

"I don't know," said the Mother Superior. "I never met the man. But if he really has been living in hiding here for more than a decade, the probability is that he was hiding from his Dionysian friends rather than, or as well as, the Orpheans. Mystery cults are always prone to schisms and dissent. If he went into hiding in order to keep the parchment away from both parties, it's possible that he genuinely thought that leaving it to you would be a secure continuation of its concealment."

"Which it would have been," I murmured, "if his stupid notary hadn't carelessly broadcast his real name, as a matter of teasing gossip. I could wring his neck."

"As an officer in the Bardic Order," the Mother Superior observed, "I'm obliged to counsel you against that. Respect nature, respect life, do no murder. That's the creed we live by."

It was a creed I approved of wholeheartedly, even though I had no religious affiliation myself. I approved of the Christians' creed too, although I wished that all their ostensible adherents took those creeds as seriously as Sister Ursule and the Sisters of Shalimar seemed to do.

"And what would your creed counsel me to do with the parchment?" I asked.

"I'm not sure that the creed has anticipated the situation," she remarked, not without a certain ironic appreciation. "As a scholar, of course, I could never recommend that you burn it—and as an interested observer, I'd have to say that it probably wouldn't do you any good to do that, because no one would ever believe that you had. The same interested observer might guess that the reason Antoine de Mesmay didn't attempt to take it from you is that he'd rather you were a target for the Dionysians than him. Handing it over to the Dionysians probably wouldn't do you any good either, because the leader of the Orpheans in the province isn't a man it's safe to annoy, if what Aethne tells me is true."

I weighed up all of that too, and thought that it probably wasn't too difficult to improvise a language of sighs, if one had an appropriate incentive.

"Is there any mention in the legend of black snow or pillars of fire?" I asked.

"Not in the versions I've read," she replied. "Why do you ask?"

"Because portentous prophecies about appointed times for great deeds usually come with signs attached, and as we have the signs, I thought that time might have arrived for the ritual charming of death to be attempted."

"What signs?" she asked.

I stood up and went to fetch her cloak from the peg in the hall. Holding it up before her, I brushed my hand down the sleeve. As expected, it came away dirty,

"Black snow," I said. "And at least a couple of the boats that docked in the harbor this morning brought back rumors of a pillar of fire sprouting from the sea way out in the Ocean."

That, at least, was something I had known and she had not. "That's odd," was her only comment, though.

"Odd, indeed," I confirmed.

At that moment, the door opened, and Jean-Jacques came in, having returned from the old Toustain house, as instructed, at dusk.

He was not alone. Mariette and Elise were with him, along with a man who had to be Charles Parenot, the haunted painter of Martyr's Mount.

As Hecate had pointed out to me, when catching me out in a trivial lie, I fit the standard image of a mature, established and experienced painter very well: distinguished rather than conventionally handsome, a trifle stout, sober, fastidious and utterly confident. Charles Parenot, still at the younger end of the spectrum, was completely different: handsome without being distinguished, slender, excitable, a trifle unkempt and anxious. He was also pale, blue-eyed and fair-haired—three more features that he did not share with me...or with his adopted daughter.

Enthusiastic as I was to meet my neighbor, rival and potential friend, however, I cursed the interruption. Accepting the inevitably, though, I simply handed the Sister's cloak to Jean-Jacques, telling him to hang it up again, and got ready to make the introductions.

IX. The Child Prodigy

Jean-Jacques took the cloak, but immediately dissolved into apologies, excusing his indiscreet intrusion on the grounds that he had had no idea that I was not alone. I accepted his apology and told him to instruct Luzon to make a large pot of tea, and then, as there was still no fire in the drawing room, to fetch some extra chairs, so that we could all sit around the studio fire.

Then it was Charles Parenot's turn to apologize for disturbing us, excusing his intrusion on the grounds of the extreme gratitude he wasted to express for my lending him my servants to help him bring some order to his new residence.

After that, of course, it was my turn, apologizing for the mess in the studio and the absence of a fire in the drawing room, excusing myself on the grounds that I hadn't been expecting visitors.

Eventually, Parenot and I got around to shaking hands formally, and then I was finally able to make the introductions: "Sister Ursule, Mother Superior of the Convent of the Sisters of Shalimar; Monsieur Charles Parenot, painter, his wife, Mariette and his daughter Elise."

Jean-Jacques, who was bringing in the chairs by then, nearly dropped them in astonishment when he heard the name of my unexpected visitor. The newcomers, who had little or no idea of how remarkable her presence was, took it in their stride.

"Monsieur Parenot's painting of his wife as Eurydice is hanging in Monsieur de Mesmay's small reception room," I told Sister Ursule, for the sake of having something to say.

The Mother Superior looked at Mariette with interest, and then at Elise. Her failure to notice any resemblance was almost tangible.

Everyone sat down except Elise, whose curiosity had been attracted by the triptych near the window. She drifted away, her expression still unreadable. I presumed that she was still uneasy and a little shy, but trying to overcome both.

"It's all right," Charles Parenot assured me. "She's lived in an artist's studio all her life—she won't touch anything, and she has a real interest in and appreciation of art."

I nodded, not entirely satisfied by the reassurance—but Elise was twelve years old, after all, not an irresponsible infant. I kept an eye on her anyway.

"You shouldn't have walked here in this dreadful weather," I told them. "I'll get Jean-Jacques to take you back in the carriage—and you, Sister, to the Convent. You can't possibly go out on foot again while it's snowing like this."

"The weather is remarkably hostile," Charles Parenot remarked. "Your manservant tells me that a pillar of fire has been seen out at sea. I hadn't expected the elements to go to such lengths to greet us—is it a warning, do you think?" He was joking, but there was an evident unease beneath his humor.

How, I wondered, had Jean-Jacques got hold of that information? He had probably run errands for his temporary masters in the course of the day, though, and he had had specific orders from me to keep his ears open.

"It's unfortunate," I said to Parenot. "Hopefully, the weather will clear up soon, and you'll see us as we really are."

"Thanks to your servants, we've managed to render the house habitable," Mariette put in. "I'm sure I can cope with it, even though it's larger than our little house in the capital."

"I'm truly sorry that I didn't introduce myself yesterday evening," Parenot said, "But I have so much fragile equipment that I had to supervise the unloading of the lighter and the packing of the cart myself. You'll understand, I'm sure, Master Rathenius."

"Absolutely," I assured him. "I hope you'll be happy here, and that you'll find it an inspiring location in which to paint. As you've already had an overabundant opportunity to see, it's a good deal closer to raw nature and the roots of mythology than the Capital."

"I'm sure the change of scene will to me good," said Parenot. "I'm thinking of branching out from mythological painting, and tackling a wider range of subjects."

"I fear that I'm only just beginning to dabble in it," I said, nodding my head toward the triptych, invisible from where we were sitting because the backs of the panels were turned toward us. Elise was still studying it from the other side. "What do you think, Elise?" I asked.

"I can't see Eurydice," she replied.

"She's in the crowd," I said, "but there's nothing in particular to designate her; for the moment, she's just one of the shades.

"But she isn't in the first painting at all," she observed, "and she's hardly visible in the third, if you don't know where to look."

It was news to me that she was visible in the third at all. Obviously, I didn't know where to look. I stood up and went to join her. "The thing is, you see," I tried to explain, party addressing Parenot, Mariette and Sister Ursule as well as the child, "that I'm not at all sure that Eurydice is as important as the popular versions of the myth make out, and I can't quite make up my mind about the underlying significance of Orpheus' excursion to the Underworld. But where can you see her in the sketch?"

"Reflected in Orpheus' eyes, of course," she said, as if it were the most natural observation in the world.

Orpheus' dead eyes were just two smudges of charcoal. There was nothing reflected there... or was there? Sometimes, if you look with sufficient imagination, smudges can suggest forms, like wisps of smoke or cloud. For a moment, I wondered whether Eurydice really could be seen reflected in Orpheus' dead eyes—and whether, if so, I had put her there, unwittingly.

Then I rejected the ideas and said something to myself, silently, that I had never imagined that I would ever say, so heretical was it in the context of my own private creed: *That child has too much imagination.*

Immediately, I apologized to her, silently, for the inaudible insult. Of course she did not have, and could not possibly have, too much imagination.

Aloud, to cover up the internal monologue, I said: "I hear you play the violin?"

"I used to," she said. "I have a new instrument now."

I knew that it couldn't be the marine trumpet; she wasn't yet tall enough. "What is it?" I asked, reflexively.

"It's like a violin but larger," she said. "Charles calls it a viola da gamba." *She calls him Charles, not Father*, I noted.

"I have a friend who's learning to play the marine trumpet," I told her. "That's like a violin too, but much longer, with only one string.

"Then why is it called a trumpet?" she asked.

"It's a kind of joke," I said. "Do you think that... Charles would allow me to paint your portrait when I've finished my triptych?"

I was currying favor, although I wasn't quite sure why—perhaps trying to conjure up the delighted expression she's taken on the previous evening when I'd mentioned the possibility.

"Of course," she said, "if I want him to."

I met Mariette' gaze at that moment. I could see clearly enough that she was no better disposed to the idea now than she had been previously—but I guessed, too, that what Elise had said was precisely true. Charles would permit whatever she wanted him to permit. And I understood the dimensions of Mariette's unhappy anxiety a little more clearly.

Sister Ursule began making polite conversation with Parenot while they sipped the tea that Jean-Jacques had just brought in. Mariette did not join in; she was watching Elise and me, with an attention that was slightly discomfiting.

"Come and have some tea," I said to the girl. "I'll show you round the studio properly another time, when the light's better," It was probably not the most diplomatic of remarks, and I looked at Mariette, trying to radiate harmlessness and reassure her that I had no evil designs whatsoever on Elise, or anyone else.

As we walked past the table, Elise stopped. The accursed parchment was still there, on open view, practically begging to be stolen. Elise looked down at it, peering carefully in the dim light.

"It's supposed to be suspiric language," I told her, for the sake of something to say.

She nodded her head. "I see," she said. "I wondered. I thought it might be music."

"Why did you think that?" I asked.

"I don't know," she said. "But I can see that you're right: it's the language of sighs." Obviously she had a little Latin too. And a great deal of imagination. Perhaps, in spite of the heresy of the notion and my recent recantation of that heresy, too much.

We sat down, and drank tea. It was very civilized. None of the other guests realized how bizarre it was that we were sitting there, having a civilized cup of tea with the Mother Superior of a Bardic Order, who had emerged from her seclusion to warn a reputed sorcerer that members of the Cult of Dionysus might try to assassinate him in order to take possession of a fake document.

"By the way," I said to Sister Ursule, still searching for something innocuous to say, "how is Hecate coming along with her lessons on the marine trumpet?"

Sister Ursule looked me in the eyes. "Are you a true friend?" she asked, still with a slight glint of ironic humor in her gray eyes.

"Of course."

"In that case, I can probably tell you the truth. She's making every effort, poor dear, but she'll never be able to play it. Her mind has a fine sense of poetic harmony, but somehow, it won't connect with her fingers. She has no talent for it, I fear. I'm trying to find a way to tell her that without disappointing her too badly."

"Oh," I said, genuinely disappointed on Hecate's behalf. "She wanted to accompany herself when she recites her *Eurydice's Lament*."

"She told us about that," Elise put in. "I'll accompany her, if she likes, on the viola. I'd like that."

Once again, I could see that Mariette didn't.

"Do you perform in public, then?" I asked.

"Oh yes," she said. "People were always coming to hear me in the Capital."

"That's not what Master Rathenius means, Elise," said Mariette. "He doesn't mean playing to friends, he means playing a formal concert."

"I can do that," said Elise, apparently with complete self-confidence. "I've played for the Duc de Dellacrusca, and everyone on the Mount says that he's the devil incarnate. He liked me, though—I could tell."

"Dellacrusca's visited your studio?" I said to Parenot.

"Myrica brought him," he said. "She's trying to persuade him to give me a commission. Apparently she once persuaded him to commission you to paint his sons. He seemed markedly hostile at first, although he's obviously listened to Myrica's argument that it was time to obtain a more up-to-date picture of the twins for the family gallery, but Elise is right. When he heard her play, he softened up considerably, and complimented us on having such a beautiful and talented child."

"I didn't really like the way he did it, though," Mariette put in. "He can send shivers down your spine even when he's trying to be pleasant—especially then, in fact. At least when he was looking daggers at me I felt that he was being honest."

"Well," I said, "If anyone can get a commission out of him, it's Myrica. She did it for me, in spite of the fact that he obviously didn't like me at all—although he might have thought that sending the terrible twins to sit for me was the worst punishment he could think of. They're a lot better now they're older, mind, and I doubt that they'll give you any trouble if he sends them to you."

"He said he might get Father to paint me instead," Elise put in.

"I think he was just being complimentary, darling," Mariette told her. "I don't think he meant it."

The devil incarnate paying compliments to little girls! That was surely new—unless Dellacrusca's habits and tastes were even more depraved than rumor dared suggest. I shuddered at the thought.

"Actually," I said, only a trifle hesitantly, "as it happens, the Marquis of Mesmay, who commissioned my triptych, came to see it this afternoon, and he mentioned the possibility of Elise giving a recital in his house—at a kind of reception to introduce the three of you to the Island Council. Myrica Mavor has apparently told him that that Elise is very talented."

Mariette was so pale naturally that it was almost impossible for her to go any paler, but her complexion was making the effort. "I really don't think Elise is ready for something like that," she said.

Trying to score a point to my credit, I said: "That's exactly what I told the Marquis. He mentioned the possibility of Hecate performing as well—he'll be disappointed to learn that she can't do it either."

"She can," said Elise. "I told you—I'll accompany her with my viola."

"It's not as simple as…," I began to say, not even daring to imagine how Hecate might react to the idea not only of being accompanied by someone else, but by a child—but Elise cut me off.

"Is she writing her poem in the language of sighs?" she asked.

Having been caught in mid-sentence, I couldn't change tack sufficiently rapidly to say "No," before Sister Ursule intervened.

"How could one write *Eurydice's Lament* in any other language?" She said lightly. Then she looked at me and added: "Figuratively speaking, that is."

I realized that her answer was much better than mine, and nodded an appreciation.

Elise had already rounded on Mariette. "You liked Hecate," she said, in a tone that was more threat than plea. She was clearly a child who had become used to getting her own way, and knew that she could usually get it. Mariette presumably knew, too, that if she tried to oppose her, she might come off worse—and that was the presumably the last thing she wanted, if my estimate of her anxieties was correct.

I felt that I ought to intervene.

"I'm sorry," I said, "but I really don't think that Hecate would allow that. She's never allowed anyone else to accompany her poetry, in all the time I've known her. It's something she feels strongly about."

Mariette almost breathed a sigh of relief—but she didn't get the chance.

Elise, the seemingly timid and perhaps anxious child of the previous evening, was transfigured now. Something, as they say, had got into her. She looked me in the face, and said: "Leave it to me. I'll persuade her."

And I was almost ready to believe her. She was, after all, a child who had charmed Lord Dellacrusca himself; Hecate Rain would probably be putty in her hands.

Mariette was as puzzled as I was. We exchanged a glance, and for the first time there was a spark of comprehension and sympathy between us.

Perhaps I might get to paint her after all, I thought, meaning Mariette this time. But my original intention now seemed uncertain. I had wanted to paint her as herself, not as Eurydice, but now, I was no longer sure that I could see her "as herself." Just as Elise could see Eurydice reflected in the charcoal smudges of my Orpheus' eyes, I was beginning to see Eurydice in the pale and delicate features of Mariette Parenot—and I was not at all sure that I could banish her therefrom if I managed to persuade her to sit for me.

This obsession is taking hold of us all, I thought. *It's all too much.*

Jean-Jacques came in then to inform me that the horses were harnessed to the sociable, and that he could take my guests home whenever they wished.

"If you don't mind a slight squeeze for the first two hundred paces," I said, "I'd like to come with you. There's someone I need to see in town."

Nobody minded—it was my carriage, after all.

This time, I was careful to return the accursed parchment to its hiding-place in the cellar before leaving, although I couldn't help thinking that it might be better all round if someone did break in and steal it, as long as they did no harm to Jean-Jacques and Luzon.

Elise sat on Charles Parenot's knee, and there was no discomfort, even for the short distance separating my house from the one that everyone would now have to get used to calling the Parenot house.

When we had dropped them at their door, I apologized to the Mother Superior for the fact that our private conversation had been rudely disrupted.

"Please don't apologize," she said to me. "It was a most unexpected treat to be in such company. I did have more that I wanted to say to you, and I dare say that it won't be easy to find another occasion to resume our conversation, but I'd like to seize the brief opportunity we still have now to ask you a question, if I may."

"Fire away," I said.

She did. "Are you a visionary. Master Rathenius?"

I blinked. "I'm a painter," I replied. "I have, or believe I have, a particularly acute vision, which sees things other people don't, and sometimes penetrates secrets that my sitters don't realize that they're giving away. In that sense, I have a gift. But if you mean, do I have acute visionary episodes, when I see things with the apparent force of revelation, no I'm not."

She probably nodded her head, but it was too dark inside the carriage, at that particular point between street-lamps. "Neither am I," she said. "There was a time when I was disappointed by that, because I wanted to be more like Shalimar, and the other bards, and the Christian saints. I wanted revelation; I wanted the sense of certainty that it seems to bring. But now, I no longer envy those who have that particular...I can't even think of it as a gift any more. It's too dangerous, and not only to the visionary. Do you understand what I mean?"

"Yes," I said.

"Good," she said. "You can see, can't you, that that poor child is a visionary?"

"I suspected as much," I admitted.

"The trouble is," said the other Superior, "that one can never tell in advance what visions a visionary might have, and what their revelations might reveal… or appear to reveal. It might be wise to keep Hecate away from her, if we can, because I believed her when she said that she could persuade her to let her accompany her."

"So did I," I said, "even though it goes against everything Hecate has ever said."

"Hecate is more vulnerable than she thinks or likes to appear," opined Sister Ursule, "as you must know very well."

I did. "Thank you, Sister Ursule," I said. "You've been an immense help to me this evening. I believe that I understand what's happening much better now. I only hope I can steer my way through it successfully, without anybody getting hurt. That might not be easy, if you're right about the danger posed by those who might want to get their hands on the parchment."

"No," she said, "it might not be easy, and I'm quite prepared to hope that I've been misled in my inferences. But if there is danger, not merely to you but to Hecate, I think that with my faith and your artistry, we might just manage to avoid it."

Then she had to get down, because we had stopped outside the gates of the Convent of the Sisters of Shalimar. I was genuinely sorry, because she really was a very interesting woman. I almost offered to paint her portrait, but I knew that she's refuse.

"*Au revoir*, Sister," I said to her.

"*Adieu*, Master Rathenius," she replied.

And that was that.

X. The Devil's Instruments

When Jean-Jacques pulled up in the courtyard of
the Sprite, I told him to get a drink in the tap-room and
pick up what he could from the local gossip without
seeming too curious about anything, while I went up
directly to see Myrica.

I told her that Mesmay had been to see me and that
he was fully aware of the state of play with the triptych.
I also told her that he was thinking of holding some kind
of official reception to welcome Parenot to the island,
and that was probably why he and Fion Commonal
hadn't turned up to hers.

"Damn," she said. "I suppose I'll have to stick
around for that. I was hoping to go home, to get away
from this accursed weather."

"It might not come to anything," I said. "In fact, if
you see him, it might be as well if you tried to talk him
out of it."

"Why?" she asked. As an agent, she was not averse
to the idea of people throwing parties for her artists—
merely the idea of being obliged to kick her heels in
Mnemosyne out of season in order to show her face
there.

"He's got some crazy idea about getting Elise to
perform at it, and Hecate too."

"What's crazy about it?" she asked. "I've heard the
kid play. I know you think I exaggerate, but she's a real
wonder, and not as shy as she sometimes seems. She can
be real prima donna when the occasion warrants it."

"Parenot is your asset, not Elise," I told her. "He's
the one whose interests you have to look out for, and that

tripartite relationship is in danger of exploding. If it does, it will certainly damage his productivity in the short term."

Her face darkened. "How do you know?" she said.

"Oh, come on, Myrica! Even if I didn't have unusually acute vision, it would be obvious. The three of them came to thank me when Jean-Jacques came back after helping them move in. It's obvious that the poor woman is haunted by the fear of being dumped, now that he doesn't need her to look after her any more, and the child really isn't helping, by blatantly exploiting her vulnerability."

She seemed genuinely surprised. "Is that what you think?" she said.

"It's what I saw," I told her, "not an hour ago."

"In that case," she said, "it's no wonder you're having difficulty with Mesmay's triptych. Your fabled vision is letting you down, seriously. You've got it all wrong."

I was genuinely surprised in my turn. I didn't believe her. Axel Rathenius, make a mistake? Unthinkable. Although, when I thought about it, it had happened... more than once, in fact... even when the air was providing my lungs with a better quality of nourishment and stimulation.

"Would you consider ringing for one of Madame Auger's hirelings and asking her to send up a bottle of brandy?" I asked.

She already had one in the bedside cabinet that was still half-full. She poured us each a glass.

"Go on, then," I said. "Explain. How have I got it all wrong?"

"It's not her that's frightened of being abandoned now that the child doesn't need mothering any more—

it's him. He thinks she's only stayed with him all these years because he became besotted with Elise and needed her to help him look after her."

"It really didn't look that way to me," I said, after taking a sufficient medicinal dose of the brandy. "I may not be the world's best judge of men's inner feelings, but I'm rarely wrong in reading women—not that it requires a genius. Surely you only have to see them together for five minutes to know that she's in hopelessly love with him—and that she's terrified, although though she's doing her very best not to let to show."

"That might be so," Myrica conceded, "although there's more than one way of being in love, as you know very well, and even if she is... well, Charles might be the only person in the world who's unaware of it, but unaware he is. Believe me—I'm the one whose shoulder he cries on, his one and only confidante. And although I'm certainly not Mariette's confidante, I have every reason to believe that what's terrifying her at present isn't the mere possibility of losing Charles—unless she's somehow twisted it into that in order to avoid confronting the real source of her fears."

"Which is?" I queried.

"I can't tell you that," she said.

"Because you don't know?"

"Because it's confidential."

"You're an agent, Myrica, not a notary or a physician—and you don't exactly have a reputation for discretion."

"If you weren't a valued client," she said, "I might take exception to that. I can assure you that if ever you confided your innermost secrets to me—unlikely as that might seem—I wouldn't go blabbing them to all and sundry."

"I'm not all and sundry," I said. "I'm Charles Parenot's new next door neighbor, who—as you correctly predicted, to your credit—would very much like to paint his wife and daughter, and have therefore studied them carefully enough, even if only briefly, to see very clearly that something in seriously awry in that household. Since you assure me that Charles loves Mariette, and I can assure you that Mariette loves Charles, I suppose I have to assume that it's one of those relationships in which the people involved never actually talk to one another, for fear of where honesty might lead, and who therefore brood their irrational fears in silence. But something is ready to explode within it, and I'm not the only one who can see it."

"Jean-Jacques?" she queried, not unnaturally, but with underserved contempt.

"I haven't consulted him about it," I said, "but I have discussed it with the Mother Superior of the Sisters of Shalimar."

That bombshell had its desired effect. I took an exceedingly satisfied sip of brandy while her mind boggled.

"How?" she demanded.

"She was there when the Parenots came to call. She came to see me, and we were having a very pleasant chat about the more esoteric versions of the legend of Orpheus and the language of sighs. To be perfectly honest, I wish they could have left it another hour or so before coming to call, interesting as the encounter turned out to be. She was giving me some very useful insights."

"The Mother Superior of the Sisters of Shalimar dropped in on you to give you tips on the legend of Orpheus?" she said, unable to believe it.

"Oh no," I said. "She dropped in to warn me that my life might be in danger."

"From whom?"

"The Cult of Dionysus."

"Niklaus Hylne is half-convinced that *you're* a member of the Cult of Dionysus."

"Niklaus Hylne is an idiot. And I'm not as sorry as perhaps I ought to be that if my life really is in danger—which I doubt—his might be the next name on their hit list."

"What have you got yourself into, Axel?"

"What have I got myself into? What have *you* got me into, you mean. You were the one who talked me into accepting a commission from the Cult of Orpheus."

"Don't be ridiculous—you said yourself, in no uncertain terms, that Mesmay is just an art collector with an interest in mythology."

"Well, as *you* said *yourself,* also in no uncertain terms, I sometimes get things wrong. If the information I've accumulated since I said that is correct—and some of it comes from a seemingly unimpeachable source—then Antoine de Mesmay is, if not at the heart of the Cult of Orpheus, at least somewhere in its tail-feathers. And if I told you who its leader is, you wouldn't believe me."

"Who?" she demanded, automatically.

"I can't tell you," I said. "It's confidential."

She sighed, deeply. "If you weren't a valued client…," she said.

"And if I didn't need an agent in the Capital…," I said, cruelly, and left it at that.

"Well, she said, sourly, "I suppose you wouldn't keep me on because you had designs on my body. In all the years we've known one another, you've never propositioned me once."

142

"I'm sorry if the omission has offended you," I said, "but I thought it best to keep the relationship strictly professional—just as you did."

She took a deep draught of her own brandy. "All right," she said, "now that we've finished sniping at one another, will you tell me why you think Charles' household is about to explode."

I hadn't quite finished sniping. "You're the one with all the inside information," I said. "What do you think is going to happen now that they're safely ensconced in the chilly isolation of the old Toustain house? Do you really think they'll live happily ever after?"

"God, I hope so," she said. She raised a hand with the thumb and the forefinger half an inch apart. "I'm *this* close to getting him a commission from Dellacrusca himself," she said, "and you know how hard that is. I've even got him to come along to the studio, and got the little girl to play for him, in the hope of breaking the ice—and you should have seen his face! Absolutely enraptured. Believe me, the things they say about that man's heart of stone are all eyewash."

"You got him to commission a portrait of the twins from me," I pointed out, "so it can't be all that difficult."

"You have no idea," she told me, bitterly. "Artists think agents just ferry their stuff around and collect their twenty per cent for next to nothing. Believe me, it doesn't work like that... well, it works more like that with you than Charles, because you were already established when you hired me, and I've had to work tooth and nail to get him out of Yvain Deloffre's shadow. Believe me, if I can get Dellacrusca to commission a new portrait of the twins, Charles' reputation will be solid gold. Everybody knows that Dellacrusca hates artists like poison, and only commissioned you to paint the

143

twins way back when because the family gallery would have had an embarrassing gap if he hadn't. I'm doing everything I can to persuade him that the gap isn't full, now the little swine have grown up."

"He certainly didn't seem to like me any better because of it," I remembered. "I was slightly hurt by it, I must admit. His heart of stone certainly convinced me."

"It wasn't anything personal," Myrica assures me. "As I said, he hates all artists."

"Why?"

"I don't know—something that happened before my time. Nobody talks about it. If he were anyone else, of course, everybody would talk about it, whatever it is, but he's Dellacrusca. Nobody dares open their mouth. All I know is that something happened while he was still in Italy, perhaps during his first marriage—the boys are the product of his second, of course. I think his first wife died in childbirth, although why that should make him hate artists, I really haven't the slightest idea." She insisted on the last part a little too much, in order to imply without having to say so that perhaps Dellacrusca's first wife had liked artists a little too much.

On another occasion that might have seemed interesting, but I wanted to get back to Charles Parenot. "I might actually be able to help, if I knew what was going on with Parenot," I told her, quite sincerely. "And this is me you're talking to, not Niklaus Hylne. Whatever you tell me won't leave this room. But there is a problem, and you can't solve it from the Sprite, let alone the Capital, whereas I might be able to pour a little oil on troubled waters from next door."

She thought about it for three long sips, and then had to refill her glass.

"All right," she said. "I'll tell you what I know—but you must never let Charles suspect that I've told you. What Niklaus said last night is broadly true, but not exactly. Elise isn't Charles' and Mariette's daughter."

"I'd gathered that, simply by looking at them," I said

"When Charles was a student with Deloffre, maybe fifteen years ago, he had a fellow student who was a bit of a Romeo—which is hardly out of place among art students up on the Mount, as you can imagine. The other student—I think his name was Almeras—was more interested in historical painting than mythological, and he went on to Italy to study the Old Masters there. In Rome or Florence, or maybe Venice, he played the Romeo a little bit too seriously, and eloped with some girl he shouldn't have eloped with. The father sent his people after them, as Italians tend to do, and they probably pursued the fleeing couple all over the Empire.

"It's probably a long story, but Charles only knows the denouement, which is that Almeras turns up at his studio one night, ten years ago or thereabouts, with a kid and a package, and begs him to hide them for a while, promising to come back and collect them when he can—a month at the latest, he says. Charles is reluctant, but the bonds of comradeship being what they are, he can't say no. He stuffs the package in his loft without even opening it, but the kid is more difficult. She isn't a baby, exactly—she's maybe two and half or three, and can talk, albeit in Italian, which Charles doesn't really understand very well, having interrupted his own education to follow his vocation—but she still needs care and attention. Next day, Charles is in the middle of painting a seductive siren, and the kid is into everything, and it's obvious that he can't cope—so, as Niklaus said, his model volunteers to help out, and does, and Charles lets her move in, and one thing leads to another, as they do.

"Now, Niklaus isn't entirely wrong to say that the model was a whore, but that's not the whole story. She was the daughter of a whore, who had been absolutely determined to see to it that she didn't follow in her footsteps, and did everything humanly possible to keep her out of it, even though she was living on the Mount, in an environment that wasn't actually conducive. And she very nearly succeeded in that quest, and probably would have, if she hadn't fallen ill—and I mean seriously ill, nothing trivial—and suddenly, instead of being looked after and supported by her mother, the roles are reversed and little Mariette has to look after and support her. She tries hard...very hard...to follow her mother's wishes and do it without resorting to the obvious, but in the end...and then the mother dies, quite possible of a broken heart, leaving Mariette is exactly the situation from which she wanted to spare her. Until Charles' inability to cope with Elise offers her another alternative.

"Well, Charles falls in love with Mariette, but he's already afraid that she might get fed up with looking after a kid that isn't her own, and he doesn't want to rock the boat in any way at all, and he can't propose marriage because he's still living, at that point, on an allowance from his parents, who would cut him off without a penny before dying of shock and shame—or so he imagines— so things drag on while they wait for Almeras to come back. Not only doesn't he come back after a month, though, or a year, but he doesn't come back at all, probably because the thugs who've been chasing him all over Europe have caught up with him.

"Naturally, Charles doesn't want them catching up with the kid as well, so he keeps her hidden, as much as possible, and tries to pass her off as his daughter, which is surprisingly easy, even though she looks nothing like him—and everything would probably have gone swimmingly, if the little girl hadn't pleaded with him to teach her to play the fiddle. He just played it himself in the evenings, for amusement—popular tunes from his childhood, essentially light—and not very well, but even so, he was reluctant to teach her. She's difficult to resist, though, so he showed her the rudiments. She proved to be very good at it—uncannily good, in fact… and that, for Charles, was something of an affliction."

"Why?" I asked, when she paused for breath. "Was he jealous?"

"Charles? No—if it hadn't been for his little quirk, he's have been delighted, but he got a weird bee in his bonnet from when he was a kid himself, and he's never quite been able to shake it loose. He was taught to play the fiddle himself by a character who played at all the local weddings, for the dancing—it's quite a tradition, apparently, not only in Bretagne but Normandy and Flanders too. There's always some local wizard who plays jigs at all the weddings, and has a reputation of being a bit of a real wizard, although he's just an ingenious story-teller. This particular one used to tell a story about how, when he was on his way back to his own village from a wedding late one night, he stumbled across the Devil holding one of his Sabbats—if you think the locals are superstitious here, you should visit Bretagne some time and see the real thing. They aren't even Christians, for the most part, but they all believe in the Devil.

"Anyway, according to the fiddler, he thinks the Devil is going to tear him limb from limb and feed the pieces to his minions, but not at all. The Devil greets him like an old friend, and asks him to play a jig for his

147

guests, which request he's too scared to refuse. And then he plays another, and the party is going full tilt when he breaks a string. The fiddler is distraught, but the Devil tells him not to worry, and that he'll give him a new string. But the fiddler doesn't like that idea, and he tells the Devil that he doesn't want to spend the rest of his career playing at weddings with a fiddle that has the Devil's string on it. Then the Devil laughs uproariously enough to start an earthquake, and tells the fiddler that his fiddle is one of the Devil's own manufacture, and that he's been playing the Devil's instrument and doing the Devil's work his whole life, without knowing it, and that the he really appreciates all the sin and mayhem that he's been sowing for the him to reap, at every wedding in the neighborhood for many a year,

"On hearing that, the fiddler accepts the string, and plays till dawn—but as soon as the cock crows and the Devil and all his minions vanish, the fiddler smashes that instrument, and finds a new one—except, of course, that he has no way of knowing, and never will, whether the new fiddle might also be one of the Devil's own manufacture, and whether or not he might still be sowing sin and mayhem for the Devil to reap every time he plays.

"Obviously, it's just a silly story, like hundreds of others that circulate in rural regions—but Charles happened to hear it at a vulnerable age and it stuck with him, and he always wondered, after he learned to play the instrument himself, whether the instrument he was using was one of the Devil's manufacture. He always made light of it, obviously, and never believed it, but he never shook off the thought entirely. He was convinced that particular instrument was safe when he let Elise play with it, and he was convinced, in any case, that she was at least half way to being an angel, and couldn't possibly serve any evil purpose. And then, one day when she was rooting around in the loft, she found the package that Almeras left at the same time as her. What do you suppose it contained?"

She was expecting me to say a fiddle, but I was one up on her. "A viola da gamba," I said, not even certain what a viola da gamba was, except that it was an antique, long replaced by more modern viols.

"Right," she said, only slightly deflated. "It was obviously mentioned when Mesmay came up with his bright idea. Well, that's when the haunting started, and that's when Charles, even though he's consciously a skeptic, and a rationalist, and everything else that befits a man of the Age of Enlightenment, gradually started convincing himself that his daughter's new instrument might somehow be one of the devil's instruments, and might be sowing sin and mayhem in the last place in the world he wanted to see it sown: his adopted daughter's soul.

"You know and I know that she was just growing up—hormones beginning to flow—although that's certainly not without its hazards, sin-and-mayhem-wise, in a place like the Mount, where a pretty twelve-year-old is in as much moral danger as you can find anywhere in the Empire, without any assistance from the Devil. Mariette knew that only too well, and she joined forces with me to try to persuade him that it was only the house that was haunted, not the viol or the little girl, and that now that he actually had a little money put aside, they could move away from the den of iniquity and leave all their troubles behind. I really think it might work, given time, although I can understand why they're both still anxious, for the moment—Mariette about Charles as well as the kid, and

149

Charles about Mariette, but not, perhaps, in a way that make it easy for them to talk about it."

It did make sense, in a way, of their evident failure to communicate their confused and uncertain fears and feelings. "*Might*," I observed, "is very much the operative word."

"True," she admitted. "But it is all in their minds, isn't it? If Charles can just convince himself that the move has done the trick, it will have done, won't it? And the kid really is a lot safer reaching puberty here than living among all the whores and apaches on the Mount. And if you can lend the weight of your awesome skepticism to mine, we can probably convince him, can't we? Especially as there's nothing he wants, deep down, more than to be convinced... of Mariette's love as well as Elise's safety."

It was only then that I realized that she had always intended to tell me the whole story, and that all the talk of confidentiality had just been a tease, to stimulate my interest. She had honestly thought that might be necessary.

"All right," I said. "Now I do understand much better why they're both on edge, and why they're in such a state of confusion that they can't just sit down, tell one another they love one another, and get on with living happily ever after. And I'm absolutely convinced, now, that it would be a very bad idea for Elise to play at Mesmay's reception. You need to talk him out of that— you really do."

"Why?" she asked, maliciously. "Do you think she might actually conjure up the Devil with his very own instrument, and sow sin and mayhem though the entire island."

"That crop was sown a long time ago," I told her, "and I'm sure the Devil has bigger fish to fry—but if you want to hold Charles and Mariette together, in a fit condition for him to paint, it would probably be a great help to keep the little girl's fiddling under wraps, for as long as possible. If her mother will let me paint her...except that I can't do that until I've finished the accursed triptych. You really shouldn't have landed me with that, Myrica."

"Don't blame me," she retorted. "I only slave away day and night to put food on your table—you're the one who says yea or nay. You took it on because it's a challenge, so rise to it. You're Axel Rathenius, remember, the man who's hardly ever wrong. And don't worry about the portrait; I'm already trying to persuade Charles to start using Elise as a model as well as Mariette. Dellacrusca even mentioned the possibility of commissioning one; he didn't really mean it, but it'll be easy enough to find a buyer if Charles puts his best effort into it."

"It won't be as good as mine would have been," I asserted confidently.

"Of course not," she agreed, as a good agent should. "But if you're busy, you're busy. You can't do everything. You're only human."

"Not according to rumor," I muttered.

"True," she said. "Go on, then—your turn now."

"My turn for what?"

"I've told you my secret—now it's your turn. Where were you before you came to the island, and how old are you really?"

"You've told me Charles Parenot's secret, not yours," I pointed out. "You don't have one of your own to trade. You're an open book."

"Cheat," she said. "Tell me someone else's secret, then. Why was Vashti Savage so very keen to talk to you that she came to my reception and then didn't stay to meet Charles?"

"You won't tell her I told you?" I checked.

"My lips are sealed," she promised—not very convincingly, in view of the way they'd been flapping for the last half hour.

"She wanted me to sketch a face she's been seeing in a recurrent dream, in the hope that we might be able to identify it."

"And did you?"

"Yes."

"Who was it?"

"Charles Parenot's Mariette—except that I manage to convince her that she was really channeling Eurydice, since she wouldn't admit that she could possibly be channeling anyone alive."

Myrica thought about it for a moment or two before saying: "Of course—she's tried to contact Aethne de Mesmay's mother, seen the portrait in the Marquise's drawing room, and remembered it unconsciously."

"Exactly," I said. "And do you want to know another secret?"

"Of course."

"Aethne de Mesmay's mother is—or was—the sister of the Mother Superior of the Sisters of Shalimar. The real sister, that is, not a member of the Order."

"So what?"

"So nothing. It's just something that nobody knows—a secret. I didn't say that it was an important secret. Now you owe me another one—but I can't collect right now. I didn't get much sleep last night and I need an early night. Don't forget to talk to Mesmay. Take over his reception if you can, and arrange the music yourself. You're an agent, after all."

"I'll do my best," she promised. "On your way out, ask Madame Auger to send me up another bottle of brandy, would you—we seem to have killed this one."

I was alarmed for a moment, until I remembered that it hadn't been full, and that Myrica had done her usual heroic share of drinking, as agents invariably can.

Downstairs, I collected Jean-Jacques, and was on the point of giving Nicodemus Rham a polite nod as I left when he beckoned to me.

"I'll be with you in a minute," I said to Jean-Jacques, and went over to the old man's table.

"I always seem to be in a hurry when I'm passing through, Nicodemus," I told him. "I'm truly sorry. I'll stop and have a drink with you next time."

"Have you heard what the fools are saying?" he asked, waving his arm to indicate the crowded room, where the conversations did seem to be more than usually animated and intense.

"No," I admitted. "What?"

"They're saying that the Devil's come to Mnemosyne, breathing soot and sulfur all over the island—but you and I know better, don't we, Master Rathenius?"

I did, but I was surprised that Nicodemus was so confident, given that he certainly believed in ghosts, and probably in the Devil too.

"We do," I agreed, in order to be obliging.

"The young'uns never listen to their fathers," he said. "Think they were all old fools telling tall tales—but just because something ain't happened within living memory it don't mean it ain't ever happened, does it?"

"The black snow, you mean?"

"Exactly—an' the pillar o'fire. Not all old tales are stupid, see. Devil be damned. We know what it really is, don't we? Be a lot of red faces tomorrow, when the real news finally arrives."

I really didn't like to confess ignorance, but I didn't have any alternative. "What is it, then, Nicodemus?" I asked.

He cackled. He really did have more faith in me that I warranted. "You know, Master Rathenius, you know. Hekla!"

I really didn't know. It was on the top of my tongue to exclaim: "Who the hell is Hekla?"—and then, somewhere in the depths of my memory, and in spite of the choking atmosphere that was slowing down my brain, I remembered, and realized that we were indeed in for a very bad winter, and perhaps no summer at all.

"Nicodemus," I said, "you're a genius."

I bought him a bottle of brandy too, to take home and drink with his ghosts.

XI. The Devil Incarnate

"I can't be sure," Jean-Jacques told me, before I climbed into the carriage, "because they're all so wrapped up in this business of the Devil spreading his filthy cloak over the island—although why he'd want to take in the rest of us as well as the Christians God only knows—but if there are any Italian intruders on the island they haven't been anywhere near the harbor, or even the town."

"Thanks," I said. "That puts my mind at rest." It didn't, but it seemed only kind to put his mind at rest, if possible.

All the way back, it seemed to me that I really could smell sulfur on the wind, although I wasn't entirely sure that it wasn't the power of suggestion. Hekla was a long way away, although it must have been a powerful eruption, if its fire had been visible at sea while Iceland itself was still below the horizon, so that the eruption seemed to be emerging from the sea itself.

While Jean-Jacques was putting the horses away I opened the front door with my key and went in. There was no sign of Luzon, and I assumed that she had gone to bed. I lit a lantern and carried it into the studio, which was almost pitch dark because, although the fire was still smoldering in the grate, the embers had faded to dull red, and were shielded by ash.

I went to put the lamp down on the table, and the light fell directly upon the parchment containing the sixteen rows of symbols in the suspiric language.

For an instant, I cursed myself for having forgotten to put it safely away in the hidey-hole in the wine cellar, but my memory, reacting indignantly to the insult, insisted that I had, with such utter conviction that I could no longer doubt it.

Then the hairs stood up on the back of my neck, as I realized that someone was sitting in one the armchairs beside the fire, deep in shadow except for the faint ruddy reflection of the embers—a fact that was scary enough all on its own, even before I moved the lamp and saw who the person was.

It was the most fearsome man in the province, perhaps the entire Empire including the Americas: the man that some people considered to be the devil incarnate, and everyone except Myrica Mavor thought possessed of a heart of adamantine stone: Dellacrusca.

"Don't be angry with your maidservant, Master Rathenius," he said, softly—Dellacrusca speaking softly! What could be more terrifying than that? "She really didn't have any choice but to let me in and follow my orders."

That was the simple truth.

I just stood there, staring. Then he spoke the single most remarkable sentence that I had ever heard in my entire life.

"I owe you an apology, Master Rathenius," he said, "and my thanks."

It was then that I realized that any errors I had made earlier in the day were utterly negligible by comparison with the monstrous, albeit entirely understandable, error that I had made the night before.

I, Axel Rathenius, had been taken in by one of the Dellacrusca twins' pranks! I had been a gullible fool, and had swallowed everything Tommaso had told me, hook, line and sinker. And it had all been lies.

"Do sit down," said the evil mastermind. "I need to talk to you, and it will be far easier if we both feel comfortable."

There was little chance of that, but I set the lamp down on the mantelpiece, angled so that we could see one another's faces, and I sat sit down. I was still dumbstruck, though, and my diabolical interlocutor had to do the talking.

"I'm thanking you," he explained calmly, "because, for the first time in my life, you've enabled me to be genuinely proud of my sons. Tommaso did all the work, of course, but the credit is due to both of them—they are twins, after all. If you were kind enough to be worried, Lorenzo's leg is intact, and he's in rude heath. And for what it may be worth, Tommaso really does hold you in high esteem, and was heartbroken to be forced to dupe you—but he couldn't give the task less than his very best. He had no choice. You do realize that, I assume?"

I contrived to nod my head. If Dellacrusca had ordered his son to cut off his right hand with a rusty saw, Tommaso would have had to give it his very best shot. He would not have had a choice.

"And for that reason, and others," he went on, "my apology is sincere. Although, in fairness to myself, I do believe that my method of persuading you to find the parchment for me, and even to copy it for me, was infinitely preferable to the method hypothetically credited to our imaginary Italian."

At that moment the door opened, and Jean-Jacques came in, having put the horses away, to ask whether I needed anything more. He stopped dead when he saw Dellacrusca, in manifest shock.

"It's all right, Jean-Jacques," I told him, recovering my composure because it is never appropriate to show

157

weakness in front of the servants. "I don't need anything else. You can go to bed. I'll see Milord out, when we've finished."

The door closed again behind him, very softly.

"You could simply have asked," I pointed out to Dellacrusca, finding my voice. "You're welcome to the damn thing. I really don't want it."

"But that would have been much less esthetic, don't you think?" he said, permitting himself a hint of irony as sharp as a stiletto. "You're an *artist*, after all."

Suppressed wrath can sometimes generate courage. "And you're a man who hates artists," I retorted—actually retorted, to Dellacrusca!—"although no one seems to know exactly why."

He didn't stand up and horsewhip me to within an inch of my life, which he could have done with impunity, being far above the law. "Yes I do," he said, his voice becoming mild again, "and you more than most, for reasons I shall explain, since you seem to be interested. And yes, I could simply have sent armed men to recover the parchment, and commissioned an accurate draughtsman to make copies of it, and then delivered them into the hands of experts with instructions to do everything possible to decipher them, but I could not have provided the kind of incentives... let's call it the kind of *allure*, shall we?... with which you distributed them. I have no objection to using violence to get what I want, but I wanted to exploit your intelligence, Master Rathenius, and your cunning, and I could not obtain that by violent theft, or simply by asking for it, could I? I could have obtained your obedience, but also your resentment... never your enthusiasm. Do you understand my quandary?"

I wouldn't have called it a quandary, but I could see the logic of his argument—and he was a man long accustomed to working in subtle and insidious ways as well as frankly brutal ones.

"Will you set my mind at rest with respect to one thing, Milord?" I asked, as politely as I could.

"Of course," he said. "Deception has served its purpose now, and as it happens, I have a further commission for you. As a gesture of good will, I will answer any questions that I can."

That was doubtless a composed speech, as I couldn't quite imagine what else Dellacrusca might want from me, or expect to acquire from me, but I took advantage of his generous offer.

"Please tell me that Sister Ursule is another of your dupes, and not another of your agents."

"Of course she is," he said. "Tommaso and Antoine de Mesmay are the only agents I have used. I have, admittedly, fed Sister Ursule certain information via Aethne de Mesmay that I wanted her to have, but she was glad to receive it, purely as a scholar, and even Aethne doesn't know that I've been using her. Sister Ursule sincerely believes everything that she came to tell you earlier today, and her motives for coming to see you were entirely pure. She really did believe that you were in danger—and if the Dionysians knew that you had the parchment, you really might have been. Mercifully, at least so far as I know, they do not—and by the time they find out that I have it, they will need to be very brave indeed to try to take it from me."

"Fair enough," I said. "So the Cult of Orpheus has recovered its supposedly precious relic of its supposed founder, and all's well with the world. It still seems to me to be a roundabout way of getting there, and I'm sorry that you made a fool of me in the process, but what else is there to do? What further need do you have of me?"

"Seen from the viewpoint of politics," Dellacrusca said, "perhaps none—but from my own personal viewpoint, the matter is much more complicated. Would you like me to tell you a story?"

The Almighty Lord Dellacrusca, volunteering to tell me a story—that was something else much stranger than black snow...very much stranger, in fact, now that I knew the true source of the ash inside the snowflakes.

"Please do," I said.

"I was not always the man with a heart of adamant that the world believes me to be. Like you, I'm older than I look—though not as much older, if rumor can be trusted. I was, however, always a stern skeptic in the days when I more yielding in the heart. I did not believe in the supernatural. I did not believe in the story of Orpheus and Eurydice, or any of the other arcana of the Cult of Orpheus, into which I was inducted by my father much as I have inducted Tommaso and Lorenzo. I regarded it purely as a political organization, a network of influence and control. I have always treated it as such and used it as such, regarding the ritual aspects of its conduct as mummery, of purely symbolic value and effect—much, I suspect, as the priests of many other religions regard their cults, while exploiting the true faith of those gullible enough to believe, and those unfortunate enough to experience visions compelling belief.

"The Dionysians, of course, have one advantage over us in regard to the visionary aspects of their creed, although it is something of a double-edged sword. Like the Bards of the old Druidic religion, although the modern version seems largely purged of the habit, the Dionysians make free use of psychotropic drugs and hypnosis to induce altered states of consciousness, including visions. We have always been more inclined to use music as a means of influencing minds, which is intrinsically more subtle and refined, and arguably far less effective. Inconveniently, in order to be effective at all it requires performers of great innate ability—rare ability. You are, of course, familiar with that; my informants tell me that you save long had a great respect for the quasi-magical powers of music, and some experience thereof."

"Yes, I have," I confirmed.

"And that is one of the reasons why I still need you. You understand my problem, and you probably have a deeper understanding of it than most musicians, precisely because you can look at the matter from outside, clinically. You have, I know, staged more than one musical performance yourself designed to have a quasi-magical effect, with varying degrees of success."

As he knew that, there was no need to confirm it. I waited to see where he was going, although I was beginning to get an inkling.

"Suddenly, he changed tack. "You do realize, don't you, Master Rathenius, that although I have the reputation of treating my boys very sternly, I love them dearly?"

"I have always assumed so," I conceded, although it wasn't true—and I certainly didn't think that what Dellacrusca meant by "love" was what I thought the word ought to mean, in an ideal world.

"Did you know that I also had a child by my first marriage?"

"I had only heard that our first wife died in childbirth. I had assumed that the child had died too."

"She didn't. My wife—whom I also loved very dearly, by the way—died, but the girl to whom she gave

161

birth did not. I will not ask you, Master Rathenius, whether you can imagine how much I loved that child, because I am convinced that you cannot, even if, at some time in your reputedly extensive past, you have had children of your own. Take it from me that my adamantine heart loved that girl with a determination and firmness of which no softer substance would ever have been capable. But I will ask you to try to imagine the anxiety I had as result of her mother's death, and how carefully I tried to protect her. Will you try to imagine that for me? Because I want you to understand my predicament—I really do."

"Yes," I said. "I think I can understand that."

"You might also imagine that I was excessive in my precaution, just as you probably imagine that I am excessive in the discipline that I have tried to force upon Tommaso and Lorenzo—and I accept that you might perhaps be right. It is important that you believe that acceptance, because it will enable you to understand why I feel partly responsible for what happened. I do understand that the excess of my protection might actually have caused its failure, by making the poor girl feel so imprisoned that her dearest wish became to break away from it, to be free of my confining love. You can understand that, can't you?"

The teasing finally had its effect, and I saw where he was going. I saw it all, and realized the horrible enormity of it—and the horrible confusion of it.

"She ran away," I said, flatly. "She eloped with an artist. An artist named Almeras."

"Now that," he said, in a voice hardly above a whisper, "is truly impressive. Your reputation does not belie your talent. How on earth do you know his name?"

"Myrica Mavor told me a couple of hours ago," I said, realizing that I was breaking my promise to keep what she'd told me absolutely confidential, but figuring that no promise could remain unbreakable in the face of Dellacrusca, and in the circumstances in which he and I now found ourselves. "She told me the story of your first wife, insofar as she knew it—which was very slightly—and she told me another, not having any idea, because she only knew the first slightly, that the second might have any connection with it. You provided the connection, and let me know that the two stories were the same one. So now I know why you hate artists... and portrait painters in particular. I assume that I remind you of Monsieur Almeras... and that you still have the portrait you commissioned Almeras to produce of your daughter?"

"You do remind me of him," he confirmed. "In terms of your reputation, that is—he was far better looking."

I decided not to take offence at that. For the moment, at least, I was ahead of the game. "And now I know why it had such a marked effect on you when Myrica persuaded you, doubtless reluctantly, to visit Charles Parenot while she was trying to talk you into commissioning a new portrait of the twins," I went on. "You couldn't recognize your granddaughter, of course—but you could and did recognize your daughter's antique viola da gamba. Was it a gift that you had given her?"

"Truly remarkable," Dellacrusca repeated. "I'm glad to see that I haven't underestimated you. I thought it was a miracle when Madame Mavor guided me, in spite of myself, to the child, for whom my own agents had been searching fruitlessly for twelve years—but the miracle was only just beginning, was it not? Go on, please, Master Rathenius. Tell me more."

I went on, as requested, feeling that I was being called upon to play the performance on my life. "I won't ask what happened to poor Almeras," I said, "because I can guess—but obviously, it happened before he could tell your... agents where he had hidden the child. Nevertheless, you found her again, in the end, by sheer luck rather than judgment. She's *your* granddaughter, as you say, or at least as you doubtless think of her. But a granddaughter isn't like a piece of parchment; she isn't something you can simply *take back*, once you've found it. In order to get her back, in any meaningful sense, you have to do far more than take possession of her person. You have to win over her mind and soul—which you conspicuously failed to do with her mother, in spite of your best efforts. And there are complications: Charles Parenot and Mariette, to name but two—the people she loves as if they were her mother and father, even though they're not."

"Very good," said the man with the heart of stone, who could and had ordered people killed with complete impunity, and had doubtless had no compunction about shedding blood himself when required. I knew now what commission he had in mind for me. I was to be his messenger, the bearer of the bad news.

"And the further complications?" Dellacrusca added, seemingly genuinely interested in probing the full extent of my intuition, now that I had demonstrated its capability.

"The music," I said. "Orpheus... and Eurydice. As you put it, the *quasi-magical* music, which can affect hearts and minds... and perhaps work miracles, in the right circumstances... which you're hoping to create, at Mesmay's reception, with Elise's aid. I don't suppose that even you can organize the eruption of volcanoes, however, so I assume that Hekla's eruption is a pure co-incidence"

"Not entirely pure," he said. "No, I couldn't possible arrange to have the volcano erupt, but when I heard that it had erupted, and spectacularly—receiving the news well ahead of anyone on the island, by means that are supposedly secret, but have nothing supernatural about them, it immediately occurred to me that its effects, which will extend over a good many days and weeks yet, if not years, might provide the ideal backdrop for the recovery and employment of the suspiric parchment. I already knew that you had it, but you didn't know that you had it, and I hadn't previously felt that there was any urgency about recovering it, give that no one else knew either. Loosening Guillot's tongue and sending Tommaso to play his prank were moves improvised in a hurry, but they were not without a certain style, I think."

"Did you also arrange for the haunting of Parenot's house on Martyr's Mount?"

"I wish I could say yes, but that is a complication that I did not contrive, and of whose significance I am far from certain. At first it seemed irrelevant, or even unwelcome, but then... I had, of course, originally intended to take possession of Elise in the Capital, employing Madame Mavor as an intermediary, but when she told me that she had finally persuaded Parenot to move to the island by negotiating the purchase of the Toustain house, the coincidence was so striking that I almost believed that there was more to it than mere chance—and it did not take long for me to see the potential for turning the complication into a convenience. Everything seemed to be coming together neatly, of its own accord. I am not yet ready to concede that there is anything supernatural in that, but I am prepared to admit that it is... puzzling.

"Thanks to that real or imagined haunting, you now have the great advantage of immediate and natural access to the Parenot household—hence my desire to extend your service with a further commission. You must understand that in saying this, I am not asking you to do anything that will offend your conscience. I do not intend any harm to anyone. Quite the contrary; all I want you to do is to help me to do the most good, for everyone concerned."

I didn't believe a word of the last affirmation, of course, but I did believe that his judgment was accurate, and that I was a better messenger than anyone else to whom he could have delegated the role—even though I did not relish it in the least. That, I knew, would increase his pleasure in obliging me to do it. He hated artists, and me in particular. He was deriving real pleasure from playing cat and mouse with me.

I promised him my full cooperation. I didn't suppose that he would believe me, but he thought it politic to pretend.

"Good," he said. "You will explain to Parenot and his whore all the things that I have just explained to you and you have explained to me. I intend to take the child after Mesmay's reception, after she has shown what she can do, if anything. They must cooperate fully, and so must she. As you say, taking possession of a child is much more difficult and delicate than taking possession of a mere piece of parchment. I want to you do your utmost to smooth the process. I have every confidence in your ability to do that."

Perhaps he did—but that didn't alter the fact that his principal motive for forcing me to be his messenger was that he was punishing me, because he couldn't punish Almeras.

"I'll try to smooth things," I said dully, "although my efforts really won't be necessary, Charles and Mariette know who you are; they know they can't oppose you. The law is on your side—not that it matters, since you're above it."

He smiled, not pleasantly.

"Good," he said. "Now tell me about Orpheus and Eurydice, and why Eurydice's lament has suddenly become so loud in this strange community of yours."

I knew that he wasn't just making small talk. It was something that puzzled him, and he really thought that I might be able to provide some clarification. Nevertheless, I hedged. "As the leader of the Orphean cult, at least in the province, and perhaps throughout the Empire," I countered, "You're surely in a better position to answer that question than I can."

"Do you think so?" he said. "No, of course you don't—you think you understand all these matters far better than anyone else, because you're an *artist*." He practically spat the last word out. "And in any case, Sister Ursule, with a little prompting from Antoine, via Aethne, has doubtless already explained to you the core of the supposed occult knowledge of the ancient Cult, which ceased to be truly occult a long time ago, at least with regard to conscientious scholars. So stop prevaricating, please, and tell me your version of the myth and its meaning, your version of what the parchment contains, and your estimation of its value, if any."

XII. The Deadline

"Do you mind if we put the theoretical discussion off until tomorrow?" I asked, boldly. "I was up all last night copying your parchment for you, and I could really do with some sleep."

"Yes," he said, "I do mind. Time is of the essence. Tomorrow night, Madame Savage will be holding a séance at the Marquis de Mesmay's house, and although I am certain that there will be no authentic supernatural manifestations, I am still interested to hear what she has to say, and if she does imagine that she is channeling Eurydice, I want to be able to put what she says in context."

It didn't surprise me that Dellacrusca knew what I had communicated to Vashti only a little more than twenty-four hours earlier. Nothing is truly secret in houses where there are servants.

"Who else will be present?" I asked, although I could guess,

"Vashti will invite your friend Hecate Rain—and the Marquis will, of course, invite Charles and Mariette. You're very welcome to attend yourself, and I hope you will. Elise will be there, but not as a participant in the séance. Her turn will come two days later, when the Marquis hosts his reception, and she will play the viol. Hecate Rain will also be invited to perform—and again, I hope that you will be present."

There was no point at all in my telling him that I didn't think it was a good idea. He had decided.

"I suppose you'd like me to put the triptych on exhibition as well?" I queried.

"Certainly, if you can finish it in time," he said. "Although I must admit that you're further behind than I'd hoped. Still—miracles can be achieved when the spur of inspiration stabs. It's not essential, though. The only essential thing is that Elise plays. I want to hear and savor the artistry of my own flesh and blood, magical or not. And I want her to know who she really is—and welcome the revelation"

"You wouldn't consider a postponement?"

"No, I wouldn't. Now, tell me: how and why is Vashti Savage experiencing visions of Eurydice? What, if anything, does it signify?"

He really wanted to know. He was convinced that the entire mythos of his cult was just hot air, flimflam to confuse the gullible... but even the most cynical of showmen can't remain entirely immune to the seductions of their own patter. He knew that something was going on, haunting the island as well as the Parenots, and he wanted to understand it—in order to take control of it, if he could. I supposed that I ought to be glad that he hadn't simply had the Parenots murdered and Elise assigned to his custody by the generous operators of the law, and then issued an edict forbidding any more manifestations of Eurydice in art or dreams, with the expectation of being obeyed.

"Vashti really does have a gift," I told him, "although it's an artistic gift rather than a supernatural one. I don't believe in a literal underworld or any other kind of world of the dead, any more than you do, but there is a sense, nevertheless, in which the dead survive in memory, and not just in the trivial sense that the living people who knew them remember them consciously. Our consciousness is only a part of ourselves, less capacious and less powerful than we like to believe. Much of our motivation comes from the unconscious part of our minds, which lies, by definition, beyond the scope of our apprehension and reason."

"I know all that," Dellacrusca said with a hunt of impatience. "Get to the point."

I knew that he didn't know as much as he thought, and certainly didn't understand as much as he thought, but he was setting the deadlines, so I stepped up the pace, while resolutely maintaining the line of the argument.

"Although we can't know, directly, what the contents of the unconscious mind are," I said, "things can and do emerge from it, continually, in the form of images, which provide much of the substance of dreams, much of the substance of myth, and much of the substance of art. We don't usually understand them, and perhaps we can't really understand them, because our intelligence is too limited, but we can influence them, operate upon them, and summon them—at least, some of us can: morpheomorphists, mediums, hypnotists, musicians, poets, storytellers and painters are all able, to the extent of their talent, to weave connections between the conscious and the unconscious that at least give us an illusion of...I suppose it might be called mastery, or control, although it's more likely that we're the ones being mastered than the ones doing the mastering, the ones being controlled rather than the controllers.

"So, the myth of Orpheus' descent into the Underworld has to be construed, in my view, as a symbolic account of a descent into the unconscious. Orpheus, to my mind, is symbolic not of a particular musician, but of music itself, of the mysterious power that music has to appeal to the emotions, to charm them, to excite them, and more...to work a kind of magic, beneath the level of consciousness. He never was an actual human being, in my view, although the whole point is that he's symbolic of a human ability. In one story, where he joins the Argonauts in order to defend them from the temptation of the sirens, he functions as a shield against the supernatural, but the story of Eurydice is different. It's a love story—a tragic love story, of love spoiled by death, and an attempt to defy death, in order to recover love, which can be seen as heroic, but which might also be seen as foolish.

"Classical myth is full of love stories, of course, but its images of love tend to be more various than those find in modern love stories, which are, on the whole, much more certain in offering a particular idea of love: 'true love,' in which phrase 'true' doesn't mean genuine, but faithful. The modern fiction of love is much more heavily committed than the Classical one to the ideal of a single, unique, all-encompassing love: an obsessive love, which imagines love primarily as *possession*, in every sense of the word."

I could see Dellacrusca stirring now, letting a certain irritation show for the first time—but he had asked for my opinion, and I felt that lying to him would probably work out worse in the long run than telling him the truth.

"Classical myth is, in general, much more aware of the often fleeting nature of passion, the essential unreliability of the emotions that surge so mysteriously from the unconscious—but in the myth of Orpheus' love for Eurydice, Orpheus' love is certainly represented in that all-encompassing, all-devouring fashion. The whole point of the story is that Orpheus is prepared to defy the dictates of death itself in order to recover his lost love: prepared to go into the world of the dead, to charm the shades, and Hades himself, in order to get what he wants. But he can't. In the end, although he comes to the very brink of success, to the actual threshold of the Underworld, he can't bring Eurydice back with him. He turns around; he looks—and when he looks, she vanishes, as dreams so often do as soon as we become conscious of them.

"All that is easy enough to understand, viewed from my perspective. The addition to the story of the symbols on the parchment, I assume to be an embellishment added by the cult, which wouldn't have any ostensible *raison d'être* unless it maintained the conviction that what Orpheus had done, in simple matters like charming the animals and warding off the sirens, can still be done, on a routine basis, and that even the quest to redeem Eurydice from the Underworld might still be possible in theory, given the right circumstances. So the cult's founders invented a formula—unreadable, to be sure, but nevertheless solid, that was potentially capable of doing what Orpheus had failed to do at his first attempt, given a musician with sufficient talent, and the inspiration that would allow him… or her… to read the cryptic script.

"Tommaso was right, by the way, to call the parchment a cryptogram, even though it isn't encrypted in the vulgar and trivial respect by which the symbols of a comprehensible message are substituted in such a way as to hide the meaning in the absence of the key. It's encrypted in the deeper and more literal sense of being buried, or entombed. It doesn't have a simple meaning that can simply be read by substituting letters, words or musical notes for the symbols, but it does have a meaning in the sense that it appeals to the unconscious, to artistic inspiration—and because of that, there's a sense in which it could potentially be read, and interpreted, by someone who understands the language of sighs."

I was on safer ground now—but I wasn't convincing him.

"And can it really bring Eurydice out of the Underworld?" he asked, his voice dripping irony.

"That depends," I said.

"On what?"

"Perhaps on whether Eurydice wants to come. That's what's missing from the myth, you see: it has no account of what she thinks, what she wants."

"She loves Orpheus."

"She did while he was alive... but did she love him in the same way that he loved her? Did she love him obsessively, possessively and imperiously... or did she love him in a more moderate, more fragile, more merely human fashion?"

"What are you getting at, Rathenius?" he snapped, losing his veneer.

"I'm relating my interpretation of the myth, as you commanded me to do, Milord—and doing it honestly, because I think I owe you the truth, in spite of the fact that you've inveigled me into this affair with lies, because I'm an artist, not a back-stabbing hypocrite."

That was way over the top, and might have got me killed, but I was still a little drunk, still a little poisoned by the exhalations of distant Hekla, and *very* tired.

Dellacrusca was capable of enormous self-control, however, and he wanted to hear me out. "Go on," he said.

"Nobody knows what Eurydice wanted," I said. "The members of Cult of Orpheus least of all, precisely because they *are* the cult of Orpheus, whose sole concern is what *he* wanted. Perhaps she didn't want to come back from the Underworld, even if it is the bleak and dismal place that Homer painted it. Perhaps, even if she wanted to, she knew that she couldn't, that there was no possible future in a relationship with Orpheus. Perhaps she loved him enough to know that it wouldn't do either of them any good for her to make an attempt or put on a pretense of becoming his possession. Perhaps she turned back at the threshold because she felt that she couldn't do otherwise. Nobody knows, because nobody ever listened to Eurydice's lament—only to Orpheus' obsession.

"Nobody knows, so I can't tell you. Vashti will be able to give you her version, with the right stimulus, and Hecate will eventually finish hers, when the inspiration comes, but if they conflict, as they probably will, I won't be able to tell you which is correct, if either of them is. And if Elise Parenot really can read the parchment, by means of whatever mysterious intuition, and summons her own Eurydice from the Underworld, that one will be hers too, and no more reliable. Nobody knows, Milord, because nobody can."

"Her name isn't Parenot," said Dellacrusca.

"No," I agreed, "it's Almeras. But nobody knows that, except for you, me and Charles Parenot."

"And what about the maenads?" the master of ceremonies demanded. "Where do they come in?"

"Even the myth claims uncertainty about that. Perhaps Dionysus sent them. Perhaps it was Hades. Nobody knows."

"You're not, at least, going to suggest that it might have been Eurydice who inspired them?"

"No, I'm not," I said. "Even she didn't love him anymore, she had loved him once. I can't believe that she'd do that to him. I won't believe it. It might have

174

been Dionysus or Hades—or, to be strictly accurate, the forces of the unconscious symbolized by those figures—but it wasn't Eurydice. My opinion is that however he died, he died with her image still in his eyes, and that she mourned him sincerely, even if she couldn't be what he wanted her to be. If the roles had been reversed, of course, it would have been different. Men can and do kill, all the time, out of frustrated love. They kill their rivals, and they kill the objects of their love, simply for being unable to be what they want them to be. But women, for the most part, don't. Eurydice wouldn't, and didn't. That's what I believe, at any rate."

Dellacrusca thought about that for two full minutes. Then he said: "You're a clever man, Master Rathenius, and a brave one. I was right to think that you were the messenger I needed. You won't let me down, will you?"

At least he hadn't resorted to violence—yet. "I really don't know if I can," I told him, ruefully. "I can deliver the message for you, since you give me no option, but beyond that… I really don't have any influence at all."

"Do your best" he said, in a voice of adamant. "You're an artist, after all, and something of a sorcerer if your reputation can be trusted. If anyone can work magic, it's surely you."

XIII. Working Magic

I slept late, inevitably. When I had had breakfast, I wondered briefly whether I ought to go to the studio and start work frantically on the triptych, but I knew that there was no point. It couldn't be finished in three days—not to my standards, at any rate. In any case, heretical as the idea might seem, there were more important things to be done than painting.

My first port of call, obviously, was the Parenot house.

Mariette answered the door, and told me that Charles and Elise had gone into town to make necessary purchases. She didn't invite me in, but she couldn't politely refused me admission when I simply walked in, as if she had.

I started with the simple matter. "I know why the weather is so terrible," I told her. "One of the volcanoes on Iceland has erupted. It's said to do it once every hundred years or so, but it's been a little longer, and the eruption seems to have been unusually violent. The black particles in the snow are tiny particles of ash falling back to earth, and the bad smell in the air is residue from the gases the volcano has vented, fortunately diluted by distance to the threshold of perceptibility. The effects might linger for some time, I fear, but when the cloud eventually clears, we'll have some spectacular sunsets."

"So it's not the Devil's work, then," she said, lightly, to emphasize that she had never believed that it was.

"The indigenes won't be convinced," I said. "There's an opinion that holds that volcanoes are the mouths of Hell, and eruptions a matter of the Devil's belches."

"How very decorous," she said. "On Martyr's Mount they'd be certain to invert the metaphor. Is that what you called to tell us?"

"No," I said. "Some time this morning, a note will arrive from the Marquise de Mesmay inviting you to her house tonight for a séance by a local medium, Vashti Savage—Myrica might have mentioned her to you. Then, the Marquis will invite you to a reception two nights later, ostensibly to introduce you to the Island Council and other local notables. He'll ask you to permit Elise to play her viol."

She studied me carefully,

"And you think we ought to refuse?" she said, speculatively.

"You won't be able to refuse. The man organizing the reception doesn't permit refusal."

"Mesmay?"

"Dellacrusca."

"I didn't know that he was on the island. He's already heard Elise play. Myrica Mavor brought him to Charles' studio on the Mount to see his paintings—as we told you last night, she's trying to persuade him to commission a new portrait of the twins."

"I know," I said. "An understandable effort on Myrica's part, as Charles' agent—but one whose consequences you might not like. What I was sent to tell you is that Dellacrusca recognized your daughter's instrument as one that he gave to his daughter some fifteen years ago."

Once again, Mariette's complexion attempt to attain unprecedented extremes of pallor. She almost fainted, and I was actually ready to catch her, but she pulled herself together. Eventually, she managed to speak.

"Elise's mother...," she began.

"Was Dellacrusca's daughter," I finished for her, to spare her the effort.

She finally invited me to sit down, presumably because she wanted to sit down herself. Unlike me, she had a fire set in what was obviously destined to be the Parenots' reception room, although it must have had some other purpose in Toustain's day, as he never received.

She stared at me with frank hostility. "So you're his messenger?" she queried.

"Reluctantly, yes," I admitted. "As I said, he doesn't permit refusal. Madame Parenot, I know that I somehow contrived to make a poor impression when we first met, but I truly want to be a friend to you and Charles. You have no reason to trust me, especially now, but I really do not want anyone to be hurt, if it's possible to avoid it."

"Is that a threat?" she asked.

"Absolutely not," I said. "Even Dellacrusca, for the moment, isn't thinking about threats."

"But he does want his granddaughter?"

"Yes, and he intends to take her, after the reception—but more importantly, he wants her to want to go with him. That's the difficult bit, for all of us. I hate to have to say it, but it's in your interest and Elise's to make every effort to grant his wish."

She thought about that for a few moments, and then said, presumably just to break the silence: "I'm not Madame Parenot."

"Yes you are," I said. "In every meaningful way."

That surprised her. "You haven't heard the rumors, then?" she said.

"I have, and I know exactly what they're worth. But I have eyes, and I pride myself on their keenness. I know that you and Charles are more securely married than the vast majority of those who've taken the trouble to obtain some futile official certificate. You love him, he loves you, and you both love Elise. That's a true family, no matter what hauntings have come to disturb it."

"Do you mean Dellacrusca, or have you been talking to Myrica Mavor?"

"Both, although she swore me to secrecy, and I suspect that he wouldn't entirely approve of my telling you bluntly what the situation is. The circumstances demand honesty, though, and you shouldn't be jealous of the fact that Charles confided his troubles to Myrica rather than talking about it to you."

"He was trying to spare me, I suppose," said Mariette, bitterly.

"Yes, he was," I told her. "Misguided he might have been, but disloyal he was not."

"He doesn't really owe me any loyalty," she said, in a low voice. "No matter what you say, we're not married. I'm just a whore he took in to help him look after his foundling."

"There is no such thing as a whore," I told her. "And he certainly does owe you loyalty, not because you love him but because he loves you. He understands that, I think...unlike Dellacrusca, who has a very different notion of love, in which every obligation is owed to him, and only those he cares to impart are owed by him. He's an unfortunate in his way, all his native artistry perverted by his heart of stone. But he is what he is, and I doubt that he can be changed now, even by Elise."

She focused on the heart of the matter. "He could just take her."

"He could," I said, "but he wants more than that."

"And he wants us to help him—Charles and me?"

"Yes, and me too. For some reason, he thinks that I can."

"How?" she said, scathingly. "By magic."

"Oddly enough, yes," I said. "Although, when he said it, he was almost as sarcastic as you. He wants me to persuade you and Charles not merely to accept the inevitably, but to make things easy for him, in order to spare Elise's feelings, although I'm certain that you can see the necessity without any help from me. I suspect that he's putting extra responsibility on me in order that, if things do go awry, he'll have a convenient scapegoat."

"So he wants us to pretend that we're absolutely delighted to have found her grandfather for her, and eager to send her to her true home... to *Dellacrusca!* Do you know how he treats those two boys of his."

"All too well," I assured her. "But he wouldn't treat Elise the same way. He'll even try not to make the same mistakes again that caused his daughter to run away with the most undesirable man she could find."

"Do you know what happened to Almeras?"

"Dead, obviously. I've no idea how—I didn't ask. I don't know how the daughter died either, although I'm prepared to believe that it was in childbirth."

"I must confess," she said, "that I wouldn't have been glad if Almeras had come back for her himself, and certainly not if anyone else had come try to take her away, even if they had a legal right... but *Dellacrusca!*"

"I know how you feel," I said. "So does he. That's why he's taking the roundabout route—but he is determined to get there."

"Why the séance?" she asked. "I can understand the reception, but surely Dellacrusca isn't a spiritist?"

"No," I agreed, "but he is the figurehead of the Cult of Orpheus, at least in the province, perhaps in the whole Empire. He doesn't believe in omens, but he has to pay attention to them when his followers discover them. He knows that something is going on, with the various hauntings that have been reported back to him, even though he thinks it's all in the mind. He wanted me to explain it, and I tried—but he hated the explanation. He's looking to be convinced that it's all hot air, although he can't be certain that it is. Hence the examination of Vashti Savage…and Hecate Rain, if she'll consent to be examined, come the reception…and, of course, Elise."

"Will she consent? Hecate Rain, that is?"

"I'll have to talk to her about that. It's not my decision."

"I liked her. I thought she might be a friend."

"She will be. She is."

"But he's already examined Elise. He's heard her play—in the supposedly haunted house, if Myrica can be believed; on the haunted viol, if the other explanation is true."

"That's not the test he wants her to undergo. He wants to see whether she can obtain any inspiration from the parchment that was on my table last night when you came to call. It's an important artifact in the arcana of the cult. He presumably wants her to fail, along with Vashti and Hecate, so that he can rest easy in the conviction that it really is all flimflam, to dress up their ceremonies and throw dust in the eyes of the gullible, but he really is interested to see what her music might do."

"And she will fail, presumably, because it really is all flimflam?" She didn't believe that. She couldn't, any longer.

"Exactly what form did these hauntings take?" I asked. "Myrica was very vague about that."

"Sensations," Mariette reported. "Always when Elise played, and lingering thereafter, although she didn't seem to be aware of them herself until she went to bed, when she had lurid dreams—what kind, I can't tell you, because by the time we'd calmed her down and woken them up she'd forgotten them. I was awake, though, and haven't forgotten. I can't really speak for Charles, although it was obvious he was disturbed, because he's not one for communication—except, apparently, when he pours out his heart to Myrica—but for me the sensations were annoyingly clichéd: sensations of inexplicable chill; the feeling that there's a presence in the room of someone or something invisible, distant sounds like someone sobbing and sighing. The usual stuff of popular ghost stories. I'd like to have been able to treat it with contempt, but when one actually experiences these things...once or twice I could have put behind me, but it wore me down."

"Have you felt them since you've been here?"

"No—but Elise hasn't played her viol yet. That... examination is still to come. I dare say that your keen sight hasn't overlooked my anxieties—they must be painfully obvious."

"Yes," I admitted. "I wasn't sure how to interpret them, at first, but I understand now."

"The news you've brought hasn't exactly helped to soothe them," she said.

"I understand that too," I told her. I thought I was making headway, and was on the way to winning a measure of trust, in spite of everything—but then the doorbell rang. I assumed that it was the delivery of Mesmay's invitation

"Don't get up," she said, as she went to answer it. I did as I was told.

Two minutes later, she ushered in Hecate Rain. I could have taken the view that it saved me a trip to visit her, but I could see that it was going to complicate matters in the short term.

No sooner had Hecate responded to an invitation to sit down, in fact, than Mariette said: "Did Dellacrusca send you too?"

"Dellacrusca?" Hecate queried. It was obvious that she had no idea why the name had been thrown at her.

Mariette did not apologize. "Your friend Rathenius," she said, "was sent by Dellacrusca to request our meek co-operation in his claiming of Elise."

Hecate was utterly nonplussed. "I don't understand," she said.

I had hoped to fill her in rather more gradually, and more fully, but there was no time now.

"Dellacrusca is Elise's grandfather," I told her. "He came to see me last night, to reclaim the parchment that Toustain bequeathed to me, and to demand that I assist him smoothing the way to winning his granddaughter's heart. As you can imagine, it was a request I couldn't refuse, no matter how distasteful it seemed."

Hecate's instant reaction was to throw her arms round Mariette. "Oh, you poor dear!" she exclaimed. "Dellacrusca!"

Mariette was not in a mood to be hugged. She pulled away.

"You're involved too, it seems," she said.

"I am not!" Hecate protested.

"She doesn't mean involved in taking Elise away," I hastened to explain. "Dellacrusca's... concerned about various artistic and seemingly supernatural manifestations bearing on his Cult's mythology. He doesn't really think it's of any importance, but he'd like to hear your version of *Eurydice's Lament*. You'll receive an invitation to the Marquis of Mesmay's reception later today."

"The poem isn't finished," she said, bewildered.

"I did mention that," I told her. "His only reaction was to suggest, unsubtly, that I hurry you up—but he's not insistent about that, any more than he's insistent about my finishing the triptych. He isn't prepared to brook any delay simply to let the artistic process take its course. The only thing he's absolutely determined to see, or hear, is Elise trying to play the language of sighs."

"And suppose she doesn't want to, or can't?" Hecate asked.

Mariette sighed. "As for the first, I suspect that she'll be only too eager. As to the second...knowing Elise, if she can't, she'll try with all her might to pretend."

"Which might, in fact," I observed, "come to the same thing. And if the viol really is haunted..."

They both looked at me expectantly.

"Well, what?" said Hecate.

"I really haven't the faintest idea," I said, "but if it could produce all the classic symptoms of spectral visitations in the Capital, I'd expect no less here, and given the additional circumstances, maybe more."

"You think she really might summon Eurydice from the Underworld?" Atypically, Hecate put all her reserves of skepticism into her voice.

"Perhaps," I said. "The real question is: what might Eurydice do if she gets here? What will she want?"

Nobody could answer that. In any case, no one had an opportunity to try, because the three of us heard the sound of the front door opening, and a few moments later, Elise came running into the room, obviously expecting to find Mariette alone, She stopped dead, and scanned the three of us suspiciously, as if wondering whether we'd been talking about her behind her back.

I looked at Mariette. Unless and until I could get Charles on his own, it was her decision as to what to say, to whom, and when.

For the moment, she was not about to make any revelations. There was an empty pause

Elise suddenly decided that it was time to play the grown-up instead of the embarrassed child.

"Madame Rain," she said, "Master Rathenius, it's good of you to call to see us. I didn't mean to interrupt.

"Please don't call me Madame," said Hecate. "It makes me feel so old. Call me Hecate."

Elise nodded, and turned to me. "And may I call you Axel, Master Rathenius?" she asked, with a conspicuous mock-politeness.

"Please do, Mademoiselle Parenot," I said. "May I call you Elise?"

"You must," she said. "I insist."

Charles Parenot finally arrived, having deposited his purchases in another room.

"Shall we complete the process, and all call one another by our first names?" I said, as I shook his hand.

Surprisingly, he blushed. "I hardly like to, Master Rathenius," he said ingenuously. "It doesn't seem appropriate."

"On the contrary," I said. "If Elise insists, we must all comply. We're neighbors—we must at least attempt to be friends."

Mariette's expression said that I did not seem to her to have proved myself worthy of friendship yet, but Charles Parenot was not paying attention.

"Would you like to see my new studio, Master Rathenius?" he asked, conveniently.

"I would," I said. "It's always good to know what the up-and-coming generation are doing, lest we ancients get left too far behind."

Once we were in his studio, however I dropped the act, unable to keep it up out of Elise's earshot.

"I'm sorry, Charles," I said. "This isn't exactly a social call. I brought bad news, I fear, Mariette is informed, but it's perhaps best for both of you if I don't leave the burden of telling you to her. I'll have to be blunt, I fear. Elise's grandfather has recognized her, and intends to claim her. He wants to do so with a minimum of anguish, but there's no way of changing his mind. It's Dellacrusca, alas."

Once again, I was subjected to the kind of glare normally reserved for discovering a scorpion in one's shoe. Being a bearer of bad news never adds to one's popularity.

"Dellacrusca is Elise's grandfather?" he repeated, with appropriate incredulity.

"I fear so. When Myrica brought him to your studio in the capital, he recognized her viol."

"That accursed viol!" Parenot exclaimed, rather too loudly, given that Elise was not so very far away. "I knew it was the Devil's instrument. I *knew* it!"

"Alas," I said, "you're right."

"But I could have bought it," he said. "He can't *prove* that Elise is his granddaughter."

"He doesn't have to prove it," I said. "He doesn't even have to know, for sure. He just has to believe, and he does. He's Dellacrusca, and he can't be denied. You're fortunate, in a way, that he's using kid gloves for once, because he doesn't want Elise to dislike him—in fact, he wants her to love him."

"And he thinks he has a chance of achieving that? He's Dellacrusca!"

"Exactly," I said. In fact, those two words said it all.

I never got a chance to take a good look at Parenot's studio or his artwork. Elise came bounding in, with news of her own.

"I'm going to play at the Marquis de Mesmay's reception!" she announced, as if it were the best news she's ever had in her life. And then, yet again, things took an unexpected turn. "I'm going to accompany Hecate's poem—I told you could persuade her!" The last remark was addressed to me.

I was content to stare at Hecate, who had just come in behind her, arm in arm with Mariette. "Yes, she confirmed. "I'm bowing to the inevitable. Sister Ursule is too polite to tell me so, but I'll never learn to play that accursed instrument if I practice for a hundred years. So I'm going to allow myself to be accompanied, by the entire orchestra of Sisters of Shalimar on marine trumpets, and Elise on the viola da gamba. It will be spectacular: the language of sighs, reinvented for the present day.

"Your poem isn't finished," I said.

"It will be," she stated, firmly.

"Do you really think it's a good idea?" I asked, lamely.

"It's what Elise wants," said Hecate, with only the slightest hint of mischief, "and what Elise wants, Dellacrusca is going to get—musically, at least. If Eurydice can be raised from the Underworld, we're going to pull out all the stops to make it happen."

XIV. The Marquise de Mesmay's Séance

The Parenots traveled to the Marquise to Mesmay's séance in my carriage, having not yet acquired one of their own. Hecate arrived separately, with Vashti, Niklaus Hylne and Myrica Mavor. Dellacrusca brought his two sons, which, with the Marquise and her husband, would have made thirteen if Elise had been allowed to participate in the séance, but she was banished to the servants' parlor, in spite of her protests.

"I'm not a child," she declared, inaccurately, "and I'm not afraid of spirits."

Presumably, she wasn't, but she didn't insist as hard as she might have done; if she had take her protests to the extreme, she could probably have contrived to include herself, but she was in the presence of a Duc, the nearest thing to an emperor of its own the province had, and a Marquis. As a poor girl from Martyr's Mount, she could hardly help being impressed and intimidated. She was, however, allowed into the small drawing room long enough to have a look at Mariette's portrait above the mantelpiece, playing Eurydice as a shade.

I watched her looking at it, and was not the only one watching her. If she was conscious of being observed, she was careful not to react.

"It's beautiful," said Hecate, meaning the picture.

"Yes," I said. "You really haven't seen it before?"

"No—but I understand now why Aethne asked us what I knew about the story of Eurydice at Davida Amalek's salon, and stirred my curiosity enough to prompt me to start work on the poem. It really wasn't you, Axel, although it might have been, if the timing had been different."

I took note of the fact that all three of the recent manifestations of Eurydice in our little colony had originated in Mesmay's house—perhaps in this very room. If I had known that earlier, I could have told Dellacrusca when he asked me about the coincidence. I was in no hurry to make up the deficit now, though, and he did not take advantage of the presence of the picture to ask me again. He took no interest in it, apart from watching Elise studying it. To him, it was just an image of a tawdry model by an untidy artist he did not like, not a vehicle by which Eurydice might reach out from the collective unconscious to stir individual inspiration.

Tommaso Dellacrusca, however, took me to one side to apologize. "I'm truly sorry, Master Rathenius" he said. "You're the only person who has ever trusted me, and I betrayed you."

"Not at all," I assured him. "It was very artfully done—a brilliant performance. I can still hardly believe that Lorenzo's tibia is intact. Who did I draw, by the way?"

"A centurion at the local barracks. He is Italian, though."

"There you are," I said. "Attention to detail. Masterly. And you've won your father's approval too. A superb result."

"You're making fun of me," he accused.

"I wouldn't dream of it," I assured him.

He couldn't meet my gaze, so he too fixed his own on Elise, still looking up at the portrait of the woman she had always considered as a mother, even though she knew that she wasn't really.

"They haven't told her yet," Tommaso observed. Obviously, his father had told him.

"Not yet," I said. "But they will, before next time. Her father will do it. It's up to him. I've talked to him, but it wasn't really necessary. He can see the logic of the situation."

"She is his flesh and blood," Tommaso said, defensively. "And she's our niece. We won't let any harm come to her, I swear. Neither will he." He nodded in the direction of his father, who was watching his granddaughter with an expression that was almost soft.

"He could give her the choice," I pointed out. "He and Parenot could have explained the situation to her, and asked her what she wanted to do."

"She's just a child," Tommaso said, doubtless reciting the official family line. "She can't know what's best for her."

"So were you, a little while ago," I pointed out. "How did you feel about it? How do you feel about it now?"

He finally contrived to meet my gaze. "I'm not a child anymore," he said. "I have obligations now. You have no idea what it's like, Master Rathenius. With all due respect, you have no idea what it is to be in our position—what it requires. You're an artist." He didn't pronounce the last word in the contemptuous fashion that his father would have done, because he had no reason to hate artists, as yet.

"No, I can't understand what it's like to be in the position of a man like your father," I said. "I am just an artist, free to think and act within a comfortably limited sphere. I realize that there really are compulsions operating on him as well as on you, and that a loss of control over the affairs of the Empire, as they apply to its largest province, might have disastrous consequences—but while you and your brother still have some vestiges of conscience left, you might want to ask yourself whether your father really has gone about this business the right way. As you say, she's your niece—your blood as well as his."

He nodded his head, to imply that he understood.

"Are you in love, Tommaso?" I suddenly asked him, out of the blue.

He blinked in surprise, and even blushed slightly. "Chance would be a fine thing," he said, trying to be witty.

"Yes," I said, "it would. And when you are—which certainly won't be long, now, you might care to ask yourself whether your father's way of being in love really worked to the advantage of anyone: his wives, his children... even himself."

This time, Tommaso shook his head. "He can't help the way he is," he said.

"Maybe not now," I said. "But there was a time when he surely could. You still can."

I wasn't sure, though, that it was true. I wasn't sure that the education that Dellacrusca had given his sons left them scope for any freedom of thought and action, except for the occasional rebellious prank, impudent and resentful but not constructive.

Elise was leaving the room now, placed in charge of an aged maidservant who had plenty of experience in looking after children. Dellacrusca didn't come to talk to me when Tommaso went back to his brother; instead, he continued standing still, now scrutinizing Charles and Mariette very carefully. He probably didn't read anything into the fact that they conscientiously avoided his gaze. He met few people who didn't. He must, however, have judged by their attitude—correctly—that they weren't going to put up any futile opposition to his determination; that they would do their best to persuade Elise that she must try as hard as she could to love her grandfather, even if he was the most feared and hated man in the entire province.

Needless to say, nobody went to talk to Dellacrusca; nobody ever approached him without being summoned—except that, when we went to take our places at the table, he didn't have to summon anyone. Without even being invited, let alone commanded, Hecate took the chair next to him, in a position where she would be obliged to take his left hand. He didn't raise any objection, and even nodded to her politely. He had nothing particular against poets, or women.

"I shall have the honor of playing for you, it seems, Milord, at the Marquis' reception in two days' time," Hecate said to him. "I'm still working on my poem, but I hope to have it finished on time."

Even though I was taking a seat opposite, from which I could see his face clearly, I couldn't be absolutely sure that the ghost of a smile crossed his face—but there was definitely a certain satisfaction in the way he replied: "I'm delighted to hear it, Mademoiselle Rain. I shall look forward to it."

"The Sisters of Shalimar will accompany me on marine trumpets," Hecate told him, "as well as Elise, on the viola da gamba. I think you'll be impressed."

The ghost of a smile, if it had really been displayed, gave way to a tiny hint of surprise.

"Indeed?" he said, without any conviction at all.

"Truly," Hecate assured him. "It wasn't my initial plan, but the child insisted. She's very hard to resist, isn't she?"

Dellacrusca's stare was as hard as flint. He knew that Hecate knew, even though Charles hadn't yet had the deadly discussion with Elise, but he wasn't about to make any reference to the diabolical pact he had imposed on the poor painter—and on me. "Utterly charming," he agreed, calmly, "and very talented. I'm sure that she'll do your work justice."

Then the séance got under way. So far as I could tell, Dellacrusca's grip on Hecate's hand was perfectly light and casual. I couldn't be sure about his other hand, which was gripping Tommaso's. I was between Mariette and Myrica; Charles was between Mariette and Vashti. Niklaus was to Vashti's left, and Lorenzo was between Hecate and Myrica. The Marquis and Marquise de Mesmay were also hand in hand, the former taking Tommaso's other hand and the later Niklaus Hylne's. I couldn't be absolutely certain, but with the exception of Vashti and Aethne de Mesmay, I didn't suppose there was a single believer present, and I couldn't be absolutely sure about Aethne. I doubted that Vashti had ever performed for such a dubious company before, and had a suspicion that she might not be able to function without her usual sympathetic support.

The lights were dimmed and silence was demanded. Vashti descended slowly into her trace by measured degrees, accompanied by the occasional murmur and groan, and eventually began to call upon the spirits. As I had expected, she seemed to be experiencing difficulties, but she started in a relatively modest fashion, by summoning Aethne's mother, with whom she had made contact before.

Unlike Hecate, who met Aethne regularly at the kind of salon from which men were excluded almost as rigorously as they were from the Convent of Shalimar, I hardly knew her, and although I certainly would not have refused a commission to paint her, I had no strong desire to do so. She seemed bland, meek and dim-witted—the perfect wife for a Marquis—although I was not entirely convinced by an appearance that might have been deceptive.

However, the dialogue between the mother and daughter, across the divide of death, had nothing in it to challenge that appearance. It was spectacularly banal, and confirmed my long-held opinion that it was hardly worth pretending to breach the boundaries of nature merely for the sake of polite chitchat and conventional reassurances that sounded as hollow coming from the dead as they usually did from the living. I wished that Sister Ursule were there to investigate her late sister's condition a little more inquisitively, as she would sure have done. While she was relaying answers from the beyond, however, Vashti seemed to relax further into her trance, and delve a little deeper into her own inner depths; Aethne's mother bid her *au revoir*, and was replaced by more enigmatic invisible presences, from whom Vashti could not elicit anything—so she said—but faint sounds of lamentation that the rest of us could not hear.

I was just beginning to suspect that boredom might set in when something strange happened. I felt a remarkably strong conviction that there was someone else in the room: a thirteenth presence. I actually looked around, searching the shadows for a servant, or perhaps for Elise, who might have sneaked in to see what was happening—but the doors were shut and the shadows were devoid of any solid presence.

I was not the only one looking round, though, and I could see signs of anxiety, or at least puzzlement, in some of the faces opposite, including Tommaso's and Hecate's. Dellacrusca's features, however, seemed set in stone, and his head had not budged. He was staring at me, as if he suspected me of somehow contriving the curious sensation.

In the meantime, I felt the grip of the two hands clutching mine change, in markedly disconcerting ways. Myrica Mavor's hand, the fingernails of which were as carefully tapered as ever, began to clench, and those carefully shaped nails slowly began to dig into my flesh. I moved my wrist, trying to let her know that she was hurting me, but she took no notice, and in any case, my attention was deflected away from the pain by the other hand gripping mine—Mariette's—which was slowly growing colder and colder.

I wanted to let go, on both sides, even at the risk of incurring Vashti's wrath for breaking her circle, but try as I might, I could not free either hand. I became convinced that the fingernails plunging into my left hand were about to hit bone, and that the hand must be bleeding copiously, whereas the right hand was burning and blistering, as if it were gripping a lump of Arctic ice.

I would have gasped, to express the pain, but the breath seemed to congeal in my throat as I heard someone else utter a sigh that would have made my tentative gasp sound very feeble indeed.

I had never heard such a sigh; it seemed to swell and spread, extending lamentably without ever quite becoming a groan. And before it ended, another began, and another, until there were half a dozen overlapping—and every time one died away, it would be replaced by another, so that the chorus went on and on, almost uniformly, always coming from at least four different directions.

It's us, I thought. *It has to be us. We're doing it ourselves.*

But we weren't—not all of us, at any rate.

Vashti was as silent as the tomb; it was not her who was channeling those uncanny voices. And even though they were coming from different directions, as if from all the points of the compass rose in turn, I gradually realized that they had only two authentic points of origins, and that all the supplementary sighs were echoes.

Of the two authentic points in question, one was beside me: Mariette.

The other was the chimney breast: the portrait of Mariette, as the shade of Eurydice.

That, perhaps, was where the thirteenth presence in the room was located, if there really was a thirteenth presence external to our minds, capable of occupying a real location. Perhaps, though, that one was an echo too: the primary echo, relative to which the others were echoes of echoes.

But if so, than Mariette was probably not a real source of sound either, for her features, as pale as marble, seemed to be frozen stiff; there was not the slightest evident tremor in her throat of her lips. The sighs were not coming *from* her, in any simple, physical sense, but *through* her… if, in fact, they had any real substance, as sonic vibrations in the air, rather than being simple auditory hallucinations, stimulated in our minds by communal suggestion.

There was nothing in the sighs that could not have been produced by a human voice, without a little effort and torment, but I was morally certain that none of the twelve larynges in the room was producing them consciously, if at all. It seemed to me that they really did have a more distant source in the underworld of awareness—but that did not help me to determine what they were endeavoring to communicate. I had, as yet, no inkling of meaning in the language of sighs, save for the symbolism of lamentation, sorrow and regret.

How long it went on, I have no idea. I lost track of time completely. It might have been two minutes, or ten... but surely no longer than that, because someone among us would have found it too difficult to bear.

No one did; no one broke the circle of contacts, in spite of the fact that I could not have been the only one suffering pressure and pain, and presumably not the only one to be suffering both.

Eventually, the cold vanished from Mariette's left hand, and the fingernails of Myrica's hand were retracted from my flesh.

When the circle did break, and I looked at my hands—and I was far from being the only person at the table doing that—I saw that the one was not bleeding and the other was not singed or blistered. The sensations had been subjective and hallucinatory.

Absurdly, when Vashti woke up, she apologized profusely for having failed to summon the spirit of Eurydice. She alone, it seemed, had not been aware of the visitation.

All that Mariette said, however, was "I feel cold." Charles Parenot took off his coat and wrapped it around her shoulders, solicitously. She probably felt better when the Marquise had run to summon her servants, and hot coffee was brought in.

At that point, everyone stood up, in order to move to the side-tables where the coffee cups were set out, and the circle was well and truly broken, along with the spell. There had been very little conversation. Nobody seemed to feel the desire—or perhaps they could not think of anything to say. Even Niklaus Hylne was temporarily tongue-tied.

Dellacrusca took me aside, however, and said: "I would be very glad to know exactly how you did that, Master Rathenius."

"Me?" I protested. "I'm no medium."

"The effect was not coming from Madame Savage's direction. It was coming from your side of the table, and it was obviously a product of one of our supposedly-secret communication devices. As if anything routinely employed by the diplomatic corps could possibly remain secret for long! Even so, it was an exceedingly clever trick, and I still have no idea where the apparatus is concealed. Mesmay must know, presumably?"

"Ask him," I suggested. "But it really wasn't me—didn't you have the impression that the sighs were coming from Mariette's direction rather than mine?"

"Of course I did, because that's the way you contrived it. But don't try to persuade me that the whore was responsible. I don't believe it. There was far too much theater in it for it to be anyone but you."

"She's not a whore," I said, feeling that any other denials would probably be pointless at that point.

A few moments later, as Dellacrusca went to join his sons, it was Mariette's turn to take me aside. Oddly enough, she said exactly the same thing, to begin with. "How did you do that, Master Rathenius? It really felt as if the hand you were holding turned to ice—and those sounds! What kind of device did you use?"

"I didn't," I told her. "It wasn't me."

"It wasn't Vashti Savage."

"No," I agreed, but I couldn't bring myself to make the same suggestion to her that I'd made to Dellacrusca.

She looked to her right and left, as if to make sure that no one was eavesdropping. I thought she might be about to confess to her own involvement in some kind of ingenious hoax, but instead she said: "What did you mean, this morning, when you said that there's no such thing as a whore?"

I suspected that she had overheard Dellacrusca's remark, or my reply.

"There are circumstances," I said, "in which women are forced to traffic the favors of their body in order to feed themselves and their loved ones, for want of practicable alternatives. What they do is a momentary product of those circumstances; when it is over, it is over. It does not mark them, or transform them, in any permanent fashion. The term *whore* is an empty item of vulgar abuse. It has no substantive meaning."

She nodded her head and said, "I see," as if she did. Then she added: "If it wasn't you, then it really was Eurydice?"

"I believe it was," I said, almost half-sincerely.

"And did you manage to infer what it is that she wants?"

"No," I said, apologetically.

"Don't worry," said Hecate, who had come up behind me without my having the slightest awareness of her presence, having completely lost my earlier hypersensitivity. "I did."

"What is it?" I said, helplessly.

"You'll find out," she promised. "I know, now, how to write it."

"The poem?"

"No," she replied, almost as if it were a stupid conjecture. "The language of sighs."

200

It was Niklaus Hylne's turn to be absurd next. He, at least didn't accuse me of having been the non-existent trickster. "Vashti is quite the conjuror," he said. "She must have had an accomplice, of course. Aethne de Mesmay, obviously... or her husband. It was one of these supposedly-secret communication devices that diplomats and the secret police use. There must have been people on the island, you know, who knew three days ago that Hekla had erupted—Dellacrusca, to name but one, if he'd arrived by then—but they laughed in their sleeves and let us wonder. The locals are still convinced that it's the Devil, you know."

"Perhaps it is," I said. "Personally, I think it's Hades, annoyed that we're trying to poke around in his Underworld. Have you made any headway with that cryptogram I gave you?"

"I'm afraid not," he said apologetically. "Are you sure it's not a fake?"

"To be honest," I admitted, "I'm virtually certain that it *is* a fake—but I'm not sure what it is that's being faked, or how good a fake it is"

"Just like the séance, then," he observed.

I didn't know whether to agree with him or not. Was it possible that such a thing could be faked? Probably. But even if it could have been, who could have done it? Mariette? Certainly not. Mesmay? I couldn't believe it. By the mysterious thirteenth presence in the room? If so, then some fakers of the supernatural are supernatural themselves.

No, it had to have been an effort of the unconscious mind, and probably more than one, operating in collaboration. In which case, it had indeed been Eurydice, trying to surface from the mists of myth, still inarticulate, still unable to make her meaning clear... except, apparently, to Hecate Rain

Dellacrusca came over to me again, flanked by his two boys, before leaving. "A suitable appetizer for the day after tomorrow," he said. "Was it your idea to have Elise accompany Hecate Rain in the recital?"

"No," I said, "it was Elise's. She was quite insistent, and certainly knows how to get what she wants. It must be in her blood."

If he had been sure that I was being serious, he would probably have swollen with pride. "Parenot and the whore know?" he queried, although he wasn't in doubt.

"Parenot and Mariette are fully informed," I told him.

"And they're not going to make any difficulties?"

"They'll do what's best for Elise," I said. "They only want what's best for her."

"She'll have every advantage," Dellacrusca promised. "Every advantage. Given time and the opportunity, I might even make her Empress."

"Perhaps she'll commission me to paint her portrait," I said, in a perfectly level tone.

"You artists," he said, "have such small ambitions."

"I fear so," I said. "We come, and we see, but we do not conquer." *Unlike those*, I carefully did not add, *who come to conquer, but cannot see.*

XV. The Head of Orpheus

For the next two days I worked as long and often as I could on the triptych—not on the second panel, which I left unfinished, but on the third. I was wholly absorbed for the first day, but on the second—the day of the scheduled reception—I was too wound up, longing to be interrupted. I honestly thought that Sister Ursule might turn up, if not to tell me that she had discovered more about the mysterious script, at least to tell me more about her research into the origins of the Orphic cult. Nor did Dellacrusca come to bring news of the copy that I had given to Tommaso to take to the Capital, and which presumably had gone to the Capital, perhaps even to the address I had given to Tommaso, where the finest scholars in the province were probably working on the mystery, as fruitlessly as Niklaus Hylne. I might even have been grateful to see Mesmay, but he was presumably busy with preparations for his entertainment. The only person who came was Myrica Mavor, presumably because she felt at something of a loose end.

"An agent who interrupts her best client at his work," I told her, is doing herself an injury as well as him.

She inspected the severed head.

"Well, it looks suitably dead," she said. "What's that in his eyes?"

"The reflection of his final thought: his image of Eurydice." I told her.

"No one is going to be able to work that out," she said. "To anyone who doesn't know, they're just gray smudges."

203

"The images are necessary blurred," I told her, "Firstly because death is slowly eroding and effacing them, and secondly, because Orpheus never really saw Eurydice clearly. He fitted her to his hypothetical ideal rather than seeing her as herself."

"It's always the way," she said. "We women can never measure up to our lovers' expectations. Men are so arrogant—especially artists."

"An agent who insults her best client in his professional pride," I told her, "is not doing herself any favors either. And I assure you that you have always measured up to my expectations."

"That's because you've never loved me," she said. "You've never painted my portrait either—which would probably be the worse insult of the two, if I were sensitive to such things."

I didn't take my eyes off the head of Orpheus in order to study her features. I'd done that long ago. I'd seen her, not quite in the depth that I'd have required and achieved if I'd painted her, but clearly enough.

"One day," I told her, "I will paint you, when the time is right."

"For you or for me?"

"If the time is right for me, it will be right for you."

"And will you try to seduce me then?"

"I couldn't give you what you want or need, Myrica. There was a time when I didn't care about that, and there are times, even nowadays, when passion simply gets the better of me—but mostly, I only make love to women who want or need me to do it. It's more satisfying that way. I've known you for a long time. We're past the stage when infatuation could carry either of us away, and we haven't yet been afflicted by any kind of mutual need or desire."

"We're as comfortable with one another as a pair of old slippers," she said, looking down at my feet, without so much as a rueful sigh. "There was a time when I was tempted... but I was stern with myself, forcing myself to keep it strictly business. And I did the right thing, didn't I?"

"Yes," I told her. "So did I. It's good to know, isn't it, that we're both capable of that kind of self-control and sanity?"

"Yes," she agreed, not wholeheartedly. "Sometimes, though, I wonder whether I've missed out by always keeping passion in check, always keeping it within measure."

"You've had your moments."

"Not as many as you. But then, I'm not an artist. I just sell other people's pictures."

I didn't bother trying to persuade her, for the sake of polite flattery, that there was an art in that too. I wasn't in the mood.

"Have you seen Hecate?" she asked.

"No, but she's only a little more than a stone's throw away, ensconced with Elise, preparing for their duet."

"It's not a duet. Hecate sent me to the Convent yesterday to negotiate a contract with Sister Ursule for the services of eight of her best marine trumpeters."

"They'll merely provide a chorus," I told her. "The true performers will be Hecate and Elise...and Hecate, figuratively speaking, will be playing second fiddle."

"How on earth did you persuade her to accept that?"

"I didn't. Elise did—it's hard to say no to the child, especially when you know what's hanging over her."

"Does *she* know yet?"

"She didn't when she demanded to accompany Hecate, but she does now. Charles and Mariette have had the talk with her. I imagine it must have been harrowing for both of them, but Elise apparently took it well enough—otherwise, she wouldn't be rehearsing with Hecate…although that's probably the best way for her to keep calm, and think things through sanely…if she can do that. She's only twelve, after all."

"I really owe that child a huge debt," said Myrica, thoughtfully.

"Why?"

"Dellacrusca has just commissioned Charles Parenot to paint a portrait of her playing the viola da gamba, and he's commissioned another picture from him, using Mariette as a model. It's a huge fee, and the news will send his reputation sky-high. So technically, you're no longer my best client."

"You can feel free to interrupt and insult me, then," I remarked, with a contrived sigh.

"You aren't suffering any interruption," she pointed out. "You're applying paint with a rare dash, almost as if you wanted it finished by tonight.

"No, it won't be finished tonight. There's still something I haven't quite grasped, and I can't finish it to my own satisfaction until I do.

"The high fee attached to the commissions is a kind of bribe, obviously," Myrica added, after a pause.

"Yes," I said.

"In fact, you already knew."

"Yes."

"But you didn't tell me."

"You're the one who owes me a secret, remember. I paid my debt."

"Yes, but this affects business."

"Positively, it seems."

"Did you actually persuade Parenot to take the bribe?"

"No. I might have pointed out to him in passing that it's far better to preserve and protect any and all means to keeping in contact with Elise than to abandon her. They can't go against Dellacrusca, so they have to pay court to him, no matter how much it hurts, and no matter how humiliating it is. They can see that. Your help will be valuable to them, though."

"But Dellacrusca isn't going to harm the girl, is he?"

"Define *harm*."

"She'll have every advantage."

"Did Dellacrusca say that?"

"Yes."

"Well then, it must be true, mustn't it?"

"This is all my fault, isn't it? If I hadn't pushed Dellacrusca so hard, practically begging him on my knees to visit Charles studio, he'd never have known."

"Once the viola da gamba was brought out of its wrapping and out of Parenot's loft, it was probably just a matter of time. Dellacrusca must have had men on the lookout for it all over the Empire.

"Do you think he'll still be able to paint to the same standard?"

I didn't suspect her of being as mercenary as that question might have sounded to an inexpert ear. "What does it matter, once his reputation's sky high?" I said. "Reputation is everything, in terms of bankability."

"It matters," she said. "There are other criteria than bankability, even for an agent."

"I know," I said, to reassure her. "What role is Mariette going to take, for the second picture that Dellacrusca is commissioning?"

"Persephone."

"And I thought he didn't have a sense of humor. Tell him that if he cares to commission a portrait from me instead, I'll paint her as herself, and it will be a work of genius."

"Do you still want to paint Elise too?"

"More than ever. You needn't worry about selling that idea to him, though. If she wants it, she'll take care of it herself—and you'll still get your twenty per cent."

"I don't think I can get him to commission a Mariette by you. He doesn't like you—or Mariette, for that matter, although he's being exceedingly careful not to upset Elise... for now."

"He hasn't really had the chance, yet," I pointed out. "The real test, for him, begins tonight."

"He'll take her away after the concert?"

"That was always the plan."

"I don't really want to be there to see it, but I don't have a choice, any more than you do. Are you going to bring Charles and Mariette back in your carriage afterwards?"

"That's the arrangement we've made. You can come too, if you like. You're his agent, after all... although Mariette is the only one who can hold him together... if she even wants to. I've been appointed by the Devil himself to work magic, in order to make sure that everyone comes out of it smiling with delight, but I can't really do magic, so all I have going for me is hope...and to be perfectly honest, I don't know what to hope for, or even what the possibilities are. My head tells me that Elise isn't really Charles' child, and that he still has

Mariette, and still has the rest of his life in front of him, and that this surely isn't one of those wounds that even time can't heal... but I don't know. And there's still a possibility that if things go awry for Dellacrusca, or even if things don't quite measure up to his expectations, Charles and I will both be in his sights, similarly marked as scapegoats."

"You can't think he'd have you killed! You've done what he asked!"

"No, I can't think that he'd be so vulgar—but his annoyance might be manifest in subtler ways. I hear that America is becoming more civilized, though, since the Iroquois Federation negotiated the latest trade agreement with the Empire. Perhaps I'll emigrate."

"It won't come to that. You have a good many years on Mnemosyne left to you yet."

She didn't sound wholly convinced. The possibility of things going awry, and turning sour for her two best clients, just when they seemed to be going so well, would be a chilling one for any agent, let alone one whose heart wasn't made of stone.

"Is there anything else I can do to help things go smoothly?" she said. Again, it wasn't as mercenary as it might have sounded to an untutored ear. "Apart from coming back with you and Charles after the concert—which, of course, I will."

"Ask the Sisters of Shalimar to pray for us," I suggested. I couldn't think of anyone else whose prayers stood any chance of success with any of the miscellaneous gods worshiped on the island. I wasn't even sure that Sister Ursule could make herself heard. Gods are not reputed to have any great love of true scholars.

"I wish the weather wasn't so foul," Myrica said, evidently feeling in need of a change of subject. "It's still October, and we haven't had a glimpse of the sun for five days. It's so cold! You'd think that a pillar of fire would warm things up."

"I'm sure it did, locally, but all the smoke and ash the volcano pumped out will blot out the sun's life-giving light for a while yet. The winter will be probably be harsh. It will only be temporary, though. Spring will come eventually—and Hekla, regular in her habits, won't be scheduled for another eruption for a hundred years or more."

"You remember the last one, then?" she said, with calculated light irony, but probing yet again.

I didn't answer.

"Do you think that whatever happened at the séance is going to happen again tonight?" she asked, after a pause.

"That depends on Hecate and Elise," I said, "and the Sisters' chorus of marine trumpets. But I think there's every chance that it will be even better. I hope so."

"It wasn't trickery, was it? It really was something... weird."

"I really don't know what it was," I said. "Art, of course—primitive, but effective—but as to its meaning... Hecate seemed to think that she'd grasped something, but if she did, she's way ahead of me. I'm still at a loss, just like everyone else who didn't sleep through it. Some of them are still in conscientious denial, but not one of them really thinks that it was a trick worked with wireless telegraphy. Even Dellacrusca expects something more to happen tonight, but he doesn't know what, any more than I do. He's the head of the Cult of Orpheus, but he has no idea what the mysteries of his own cult really contain and imply."

"Your head of Orpheus looks a bit like Dellacrusca now you've fleshed out the sketch," Myrica commented. "That's deliberate, I suppose. Mesmay might not approve."

"Dellacrusca is the head of the cult, not the head of Orpheus," I told her. "There's all the difference in the world. Orpheus is a symbol of music, of charm, of art. Dellacrusca is only a symbol of the lust for power and possession."

"But you could argue," Myrica said, "that for Orpheus, music was power, and possession. Isn't that why he went into the Underworld—to demonstrate his power and reclaim his possession?"

"You could argue that," I agreed. "In fact, I did, when Dellacrusca put me on the spot—but speaking for myself, I'd prefer to see him a more generous light, if I can, albeit a tragic one. Orpheus, that is, not Dellacrusca"

"You only pretend to be a cynic, Axel," she accused. "You're a romantic at heart."

"I have never pretended otherwise," I said, "and whatever the vulgar might think, the two are not incompatible. Quite the contrary."

"I think you're a sorcerer too," she said, almost half-seriously. "I think you're working magic now, as rapidly and furiously as you can. You haven't lost hope, have you, that Hecate and Elise might bring off something truly spectacular tonight, and change everything?"

"I never lose hope," I said, "until hope is gone—but nor would I place a wager on success, though, when the odds are against a successful outcome, as they are on this occasion. I really can't imagine any likely event that might prevent Dellacrusca not merely from taking possession of that child, but molding her in his own image—or causing her to snap under the pressure, like her mother... either of which eventualities would fit my definition of harm. And if I could stop it by sorcery, I would... but I can't. All I can do is try to take my mind off it, by painting. And as you can see, I'm not doing that very well at present, considering that I'm supposed to be a genius. I should never have taken this commission, and only my loyalty to you is keeping me going."

She didn't believe that. Personally, I didn't know what to believe. I was just letting my hand move of its own accord, drawing on the resources of habit and the unconscious. Any resemblance between the head of Orpheus and Dellacrusca wasn't deliberate...although I had to suppose that if there were any image still left in Dellacrusca's eyes of his dead wife or his long-lost daughter, they would be nothing more by now than cold gray smudges, like volcanic clouds blotting out the light of life.

XVI. The Reception

The journey from the headland to Mesmay's house was, as might be imagined, a trifle subdued. There were four of us in the sociable, Hecate having gone home to change and taking Myrica with her. Hecate would make her own way there, along with Myrica, probably in Vashti Savage's carriage. That meant that Elise didn't need to sit in anyone's lap. She was sitting with her viola, still in its case, between her knees. She knew now that it was the only thing she had left of her real mother…except for her bizarre grandfather,

Did she think that she could manipulate him as she had learned to manipulate Charles and Mariette? Did she think that all adults could be charmed as easily as those she presently wrapped around her little finger? Probably not—she had after all, been raised on Martyr's Mount, where she would have had every chance to see life in the raw, and the scars it left.

I felt the need to say something, for my sake rather that hers, so I asked her how the ending of Hecate's poem resolved the puzzle of Eurydice's lament. It was a stupid question, but it seemed a safer subject than any other.

"She didn't finish the poem you saw," Elise told me, almost absent-mindedly. "We worked out something else."

"Something else?" I queried, helplessly.

"I could hear, you know," she said, looking up at me, a trifle resentfully. "Even though you shut me out, I could hear."

213

I thought she was talking about the conversation I'd had with Charles Parenot when I'd given him the bad news about Dellacrusca.

"I'm sorry," I said. "But..."

"You could have let me sit in the circle," she added, revealing that she was, in fact, taking about Vashti's séance. "I wouldn't have broken it, and I wouldn't have been frightened. I've lived on the Mount—I know what death is... and I understand the language of sighs as well as you do, even if you're as old as Methuselah." She was just using a colorful turn of phrase; she didn't mean it literally.

"It wasn't me who excluded you," I said, mildly. "It wasn't Charles and Mariette, either. It was Vashti. She has rules. The conditions have to be right for her to... do what she does. At least, she believes that they do, which comes to the same thing."

"She should have let me in," the child insisted. "You should all have let me in."

This time, I thought, she really was thinking about secrets other than those of the séance.

"It's a universal problem," I told her. "At some stage, children have to be let into the adult world. It's never an easy decision to make, and there probably never was a child who didn't think that the timing was wrong."

She took that in good part. She reached out, impulsively, and took Mariette's hand. It wasn't an exclusion of Charles; Mariette was sitting next to her and it was her hand that was within reach.

"I suppose it wasn't easy," she said, trying to prove her maturity. Then she added: "At least you never tried to pretend that I was your real daughter." That didn't really qualify as evidence in the same cause.

"We don't love you any less," Mariette murmured, just to place it on the record.

Elise didn't argue, but she wasn't convinced. She'd lived in the Mount. She'd had more opportunity than most children to see what adult life was really like, in its least flattering aspects. At least she was holding Mariette's hand, not turning round and accusing her of being some cheap whore who'd only volunteered to look after her so that she could get her hooks into Charles. There would be time enough for Dellacrusca to pour that kind of poison into her ears, and perhaps even convince her that it was true, even though it wasn't.

"What exactly is this *something else* that you and Hecate have worked out?" I said, trying to steer the conversation back to safer ground.

"I can't explain it," the child said. "You'll have to listen to it to understand. It might not work, though—we haven't had chance to rehearse with the marine trumpets, and they're essential to create the atmosphere of the Underworld. Hecate says that the nuns are expert players, and she's sent them all scores so that they can practice in the convent, but until you bring everyone together...and I want my new grandfather to be impressed. I want him to see what I can really do. Last time, I was just playing tunes."

"You're supposed to be accompanying Mademoiselle Rain, darling, not the other way around," Charles Parenot put in.

"That's all I wanted to do, at first," Elise replied, "But it's not like that anymore. You'll see—if the marine trumpets play their part. I'm sure of myself, and Hecate...but they might mess it up, if they don't get it... and they're only a bunch of nuns."

"There's no *only* about it," I told her. "Sister Ursule impressed me—and that's not easy."

"Sister Ursule won't be playing," said Elise. "She's sending eight of the younger sisters."

"If she's trained them all," I said, "They'll be good. I'd be inclined to trust them."

"You don't have to."

"Elise!" said Mariette softly reproachful, squeezing her hand.

The subdued thoughtfulness had worn off now; without intending to, I'd provoked her, and had brought other feelings to the surface.

"Do you still want to paint me?" she demanded, looking me in the eye.

"I believe that Lord Dellacrusca has commissioned your father to do that," I answered, in my most soothing tone.

"That's not what I asked," she pointed out, accurately.

"I would still like to paint you," I admitted, "if the opportunity arises." I could have added, but didn't, that it might not be easy to persuade Dellacrusca to allow it, even though I'd painted his other children.

"On the Mount," Elise said, "people say that Charles is the only artist there who only fucks one of his models. Do you fuck them all?"

"Elise!" said Mariette, rather plaintively—which probably wasn't the reaction the girl was trying to elicit. She had been brought up on the Mount; she was hardly likely to have unaware of how sexual relationships worked, especially in their tawdrier manifestations. Mariette must have been all too familiar with it long before she reached the age of twelve.

It was not a time for exaggeration. "First of all," I said, "I think of it as making love, and I mean it, unlike some of the artists on Martyr's Mount. But to answer your question, not very many, even in my young days—and now I'm as old as Methuselah, hardly any. I suspect that the artists on the Mount do a great deal more boasting than... anything else... and in my opinion, they'd be better off trying to make love. Artists all do a good deal of boasting, but I mostly boast about my genius—which is safe, because no one believes me."

"Me too," said Elise, "and nobody believes me either—but Charles doesn't boast at all." It was impossible to tell from the way she said it whether it was intended as a compliment or an insult.

"I don't have much to boast about, alas," said Charles Parenot.

"False modesty is as much a sin as boasting," I remarked. "A little more faith in your own genius would probably do you good—not that I ought to be telling you that, now that your reputation is about to overtake mine, reducing me to the rank of jealous rival."

He looked at me as if he didn't know whether or not to believe any of that.

"Do you still want to paint me, too?" Mariette put in, also in search of safer conversational ground.

"Yes," I said. "Provided that it's as yourself, not Persephone... or Eurydice."

"I'll be happy to pose," she said. "It will make a change."

"To be yourself?"

"To pose for someone other than my husband—and to be out of the Underworld."

We were on the verge of developing a snappy double act, but we didn't get a chance to go any further. The carriage pulled up. We had arrived.

Without really meaning to, we had arrived fashionably late. Most of the guests were already assembled: all the participants in the séance, all the members of the Island Council, a dozen of Dellacrusca's hangers—and, at the back of the room, discreetly placed behind the podium and the music stand, eight Sisters of Shalimar in their cream robes and head-dresses, patiently unpacking their marine trumpets.

There was a marked shortage of women in the audience; the Mesmays, with Dellacrusca pulling their strings, hadn't aimed for the conventional balance. There was also a marked lack of color; aware of the danger, all the women had adopted for dark silks and satins, which wouldn't show the stains of any ash that descended from the skies. The overall result was a trifle sepulchral, more like a funeral than a welcoming party. I wished that I could find that inappropriate, but I couldn't.

At least, I thought, *it will provide a suitable Underworldly backdrop for Hecate's new version of Eurydice's lament. The cream costumes of the Sisters of Shalimar don't really help in that regard, though, and they don't, for the most part, seem slim enough to pass for shades.*

After being formally greeted by the over-effusive Marquis and the under-effusive Marquise, I was buttonholed by Fion Commonal, nowadays the President of the Council as well as the island's leading physician.

"Why is Dellacrusca here out of season?" he asked me "Something's going on, isn't it."

"Nothing for you to worry about, Fion," I assured him. "Just a little bit of personal business. No matter what anyone thinks, it really wasn't him who ordered Hekla to erupt and commanded Hades to pop out of the Underworld to place himself at his orders."

"It's going to be a bad winter, they say," Fion admitted. "Some people are saying that there are going to be epidemics—that volcanoes spread disease. I don't know—there's no one alive on the island who remembers the last time it happened. Naples is a fever-pit, of course, but I really don't know whether it has anything to do with Vesuvius."

"You're the doctor," I observed. "If you don't know, nobody does." It wasn't strictly true, but it's always as well to keep on the right side of the Island Council, and flattery never hurts.

"Is the girl any good?" the physician asked. "I've seen these so-called child prodigies before, and they're usually a disappointment."

"I haven't heard her play, but Dellacrusca has, and so has Hecate. They obviously think there's something there."

"I never thought I'd see Hecate allowing anyone to accompany her, let alone a child," Fion Commonal admitted.

"Not to mention an entire chorus of marine trumpets," I pointed out. "When she changes her mind, she goes all the way."

"I've never understood why they call them marine trumpets," the physician complained. "I have to be at all the concerts they play, of course, being on the Council, but it's always seemed to me to be a sufficiently ridiculous instrument without giving it a ludicrous name. I don't recognize the players, but the Mother Superior always trains them well. I've never met her, obviously, but she's said to be quite a scholar."

"She is," I assured him. "She dropped round to my studio the other day, concerned for the welfare of my soul. We had a very pleasant chat."

"You really are a sorcerer, aren't you, Axel?" he said, shaking his head. He didn't mean it.

"It's always useful to have friends in celestial places," I told him. "When one gets to my age, it's comforting to know that someone's taking an interest in one's soul. Sometimes, I wish I'd taken better care of it myself."

"No you don't," he retorted. "You wouldn't want to be anything other than the old reprobate you are."

It would have been pleasant if he had been right, and he would usually have been right, but I was still caught up in a role that I didn't relish at all. My gaze strayed sideways, and I saw Elise walk up to Dellacrusca, and greet him very politely, and very respectfully, exactly as he would have wished. He didn't favor me with a grateful glance, because he didn't believe that I had made any useful contribution to making things go the way he wanted. No matter what he'd said, all the steps he'd taken to involve me in this affair had been malicious, taking out on me the seething wrath he could no longer vent on the unfortunate Almeras, the painter who had, in his view, stabbed him treacherously in the back.

A pity, I couldn't help thinking, *that he didn't use a real knife*. It was an unaccustomed thought, for a confirmed pacifist—but sometimes, the unconscious gets the better of finer feelings and nobler thoughts. Nor could I really justify the flash of resentment because Dellacrusca was a wicked man, although he was. What I couldn't forgive him for was instructing Tommaso to put one over on me—and I couldn't forgive myself, for falling for it.

I finally managed to get away from Fion in order to return to Charles and Mariette. Dellacrusca had placed himself in the middle of the front row of the audience, directly in front of the music-stand and the chair where his granddaughter would take up her position. Mariette and Charles, by contrast, had automatically selected seats on the very edge of the same row, as far away as possible from their nemesis while still remaining close enough to be offering evident support to their child—the child, that is, who was no longer theirs. I sat down beside them. Myrica Mavor sat down behind Mariette, on the edge of the second row. Vashti, even more discreet, was behind her, next to Niklaus Hylne. We were all outsiders, in a way; the bulk of the audience consisted of the island's upper crust and various temporary incomers, ninety per cent of whom were presumably secret members of Dellacrusca's Cult of Orpheus, or his secret police, if any distinction could be drawn between the two.

As Elise turned to walk back to her chair, against which the viola da gamba was carefully propped, I saw her take something from her grandfather, and realized, with a sight shock, that it was the parchment, now carefully enclosed in a glazed frame. Evidently she had asked him for it. Did she really think that she could read it, or draw some inspiration from it as she played? Did he? Presumably not: presumably, it was a purely symbolic exchange, as if he were welcoming her into the Cult and into the family, and she were accepting the welcome. It was ceremony.

That child, I thought, *is far too clever for her age. She's already started trying to take control of him. Is*

221

there a possibility that she might actually be able to do it?

She was only twelve, though. Even geniuses as old as Methuselah couldn't stand up to Dellacrusca. That would require the Devil himself, or Hades, at least.

I saw Charles take Mariette's hand, far more tentatively than he should have done. It was as if he were seeking reassurance from her rather than offering it. He really did need some intensive training in the art of arrogance, but Mariette didn't seem annoyed by his failure.

Perhaps it's the fact that he can't admit to himself that he loves her that keeps her dangling, and maintains her love for him, I speculated. *Perhaps, if he's been more passionate and forthright in the beginning, she'd have moved on years ago. Who can tell?*

There was an atmosphere of expectation in the hall now. There weren't going to be any speeches, any empty formulae or polite applause. Dellacrusca, the one and only architect of the occasion, wasn't going to bother taking the pretence of welcoming Charles Parenot to the island any further. This was all about him, and no one else. He wanted to hear his new-found granddaughter play, knowing as she did so that she was his granddaughter, that she was a Dellacrusca—and he wanted to show her off to his inner circle, so that they too would know that she was a Dellacrusca, under his dominion.

The Sisters of Shalimar were all in position, holding up the marine trumpets that were as tall as they were, in a semicircle behind the podium and the chair. Elise sat down and placed the viola da gamba carefully between her knees. Hecate stepped up to the podium. Unusually, she didn't look toward me for reassurance. Even more unusually, she wasn't holding a script. Apparently, whatever she was going to recite had been committed to memory.

It can't be very long, then, I thought.

Elise adjusted the position of the framed parchment on the music stand; there was no other score in front of her, although each of the Sisters of Shalimar had one. Then the child picked up her bow, and drew it across the strings of her instrument, as if to check the tuning of the strings.

Immediately, as if it were a signal, there was a stir among the Sisters of Shalimar, as if they too were tuning up.

But they weren't.

And neither was Elise, for she drew the bow back far more forcefully, playing a chord that was impossibly loud and impossibly resonant—as if it did not come from the viol at all, but from somewhere outside the room, outside space, and outside time: a chord that did not stop when the bow reach the limit of its thrust.

In fact, although she did not show any sign of astonishment or alarm, it was immediately obvious that Elise was not playing the chord at all, even though it was her hand that had drawn the bow and triggered its release. Perhaps it was something in the haunted instrument that had been waiting for the right trigger for a long time, but it seemed more likely to me that it had been something lurking far deeper, which had only been waiting to use the instrument, or its strings, as a fissure through which to flood.

The parchment was supposed contain the language of sighs, and perhaps it did—but only if the language of sighs is also the language of screams.

The marine trumpets did not strike the same chord. In fact, they did not strike any chord at all. The marine trumpets fell away, as each of the Sisters of Shalimar removed something that had been hidden inside her instrument: a dagger.

They could have hidden revolvers, or even rifles; but this was no mere matter of brute aggression; there was a symbolism to it as well as an insanity. And as everything within that terrible scream became movement, hectic and rapid but still somehow more balletic than chaotic, I realized that the one thing that I had considered so utterly implausible as to be literally unimaginable—that the Dionysians would invade the Convent of the Sisters of Shalimar in order to sow mayhem there, to carry forward their vendetta and exact their revenge for Dellacrusca's symbolic reclamation of the most precious relic of his cult—had actually happened.

The Sisters of Shalimar were not Sisters of Shalimar at all; their places had been taken by maenads. And the maenads had one simple purpose in being there: to assassinate Dellacrusca, and sever the head of the Cult of Orpheus.

The maenads were probably screaming, as maenads are supposed to do, but nobody would have known, because the whole Underworld was screaming through the mouth of the viola da gamba, and that scream drowned out everything else... far more than mere sound.

I felt a thrill of burning electricity shoot through me, but it did not petrify me any more than it petrified anyone else—for everyone was in movement, in panic or alarm... and although the Orpheans had been taken completely by surprise, they too were drawing weapons, with somewhat less concern for tradition and symbolism than their enemies.

I whipped my head around to face Myrica, and simply said: "Run!" I formed the word precisely with my lips, because I knew she would not hear it, and trusted to her to realize that she ought to drag Mariette with her if Mariette did not have sufficient presence of mind to run too, or wanted to follow Charles instead.

Charles had no choice about where to go, because I was dragging him away, hurling him toward Elise. There was no point in shouting at him, because he could not see my lips—and because he had to know, in any case, why I was thrusting him forward toward the helpless, bewildered child.

I have to confess that I didn't do that because I thought that the glory of saving Elise, if she could be saved, ought to fall to her adoptive father. I did it because my own first thought was not for the child but for Hecate, who, was an adult, and might well have been able to look after herself, and probably didn't need my help at all—but it was yet another of those moments when passion and the unconscious carry one away.

I grabbed Hecate as Charles grabbed Elise. I didn't waste a second before turning to haul my prize away, because, even though I knew that no one was actually intent on stabbing her or Elise, the crossfire might easily be deadly. Even so, I am convinced that I saw, out of the corner of my eye, the first dagger plunge into Dellacrusca's breast. I truly believe that it was not my imagination: that I actually saw the fatal blow.

Then I saw nothing more, because I was diving for the door with Hecate in my arms, who felt like an enormous burden, even though she was slightly built, and it was one of those situations when a surge of adrenalin is supposed to give a man the strength of ten.

Shots must have been ringing out behind me, but they were inaudible in the scream. Blood was certainly flowing: spurting and jetting volcanically. And the room was full of presences both visible and invisible, real and virtual maenads, crazed with Bacchic fury. I was not at all sure, as I plunged through the door, hot on Charles Parenot's heels—his burden was lighter, and perhaps he really had acquired the strength of ten men and the speed to match—that anyone behind me would get out of that mayhem alive.

Jean-Jacques had already leapt up into his seat. It was so crowded inside the carriage that I ought perhaps to have climbed up beside him, but I didn't think of it, and simply squeezed myself in, trying to slam the door of the sociable behind me as the whip cracked—probably unnecessarily, as the horses were already moving away of their own accord. Even outside, the scream was still audible—or at least its echo. The viol was silent now, but the scream still filled the Marquis of Mesmay's ballroom, sowing its panic and its terror.

The atmosphere outside was icy, and the wind cutting—but not, thank God, like a dagger.

Gradually, we sorted ourselves out. Mariette, Myrica, Hecate and Elise were seated on the cushions, Charles and I on the floor. Elise was still clutching her viol and her bow, but she only had two hands. The parchment had been left behind, on the music stand. I wasn't sorry, and I really didn't care who ended up with it, when all the killing was done, even if it was a powerful instrument of magic.

"It wasn't me," said Elise, finally.

"No one thinks it was," said Charles, "but I wish you'd dropped that infernal instrument."

"It was my mother's," she said.

In her place, I supposed, I wouldn't have let go of it either.

"I hope Vashti's all right," said Hecate. "You left her behind."

"With forty or fifty others," I said. "She was on the edge, with us. If she didn't get out, she'll have had sense enough to keep her head down."

"But Fion and the rest of the council were in the middle—and Niklaus was on Vashti's inside."

"At last half the Island Council are members of Dellacrusca's cult," I said, although it was a guess. "Even if they didn't draw knives and guns, they were fair game. The maenads didn't stand a chance, though: it was a suicide mission. They had to be completely crazy."

"Isn't that rather the point?" said Charles. He was a mythological painter. He understood such things. Sane maenads would be a contradiction in terms.

"Do you think they got him?" Mariette asked.

"I don't know," said Charles. "I didn't see."

"I did," said Elise, saving me the trouble. "The boys tried to protect him, but it was too late. They were taken by surprise."

"He was off guard," I said. "For once, he was off guard. He was too arrogant. He really didn't think that the Dionysians would try anything, once he had the parchment in his possession, even if they knew. He thought he'd won."

"And what happens now?" asked Myrica.

"You've probably just lost the two largest commissions of your career," I told her. "Maybe three, if Mesmay went down in the battle. We're all a good deal poorer than we seemed to be an hour ago."

"What I meant," said Myrica frostily, "is what do *we* do now?"

"We have a very stiff drink," I said. "Except for Elise, of course."

"We do not," said Hecate, sternly. "The rest of you will sit quietly, while Elise and I put on the performance we intended. I'm damned if I'm going to let all that work and rehearsal go to waste. It won't be the same without the marine trumpets, but we'll just have to do without."

"What do you suppose they did with the real Sisters of Shalimar?" Myrica asked. "They won't have killed everyone in the convent, will they?"

"No," I said, trying to sound confident. "They weren't maenads until the time came for them to be. When they infiltrated the convent they were just women. At the worst, they'll have locked the Sisters up. They won't have wanted to hurt any of them, and the Sisters won't have put up any resistance."

"The innocents in the hall won't have been so lucky," Mariette put in.

"Maybe not," I conceded. "Let's hope the innocents had enough sense to play dead, and let the rest get on with the stupid games. What idiots they all are! Still feuding, after three thousand years! Still shedding blood, even now, in the so-called Age of Enlightenment. Maenads, in today's world—and here of all places, on Mnemosyne! I was wrong, I admit it. That black snow really was an evil omen; I just refused to see it."

"Are we really going to play?" Elise asked Hecate, looking uneasily at her instrument now, wondering what other diabolical devices it might still have in store.

"We are," said Hecate. "We have to. It isn't finished until we do."

"You understand Eurydice's lament now, then?" I said.

"Yes," she said, "and so should you. You would, if Dellacrusca hadn't bent your mind out of shape playing cat and mouse with you...although, in a way, that ought to have helped you. You'll understand when you hear the piece. And thank you, by the way."

"It was a reflex action," I said. "I know you could have got out in your own."

"I was thanking the reflex action," she said. "Your thoughts get tangled up in your genius, but your unconscious is always trustworthy."

"I, alas, needed to be shoved," said Charles Parenot, mournfully.

"No you didn't," I said. "That was a reflex action too. When I panic, I just can't bear leaving other people to do the right thing by themselves. I simply have to grab the credit. I'm sorry."

"Tell me, Master Rathenius," said Mariette, "have you ever painted a self-portrait?"

"Of course," I replied. "Several."

"As yourself?"

I saw what she was getting at. "Vision doesn't work like that," I told her. "I can see more in other people than they realize they're giving away, but when I look at myself in a mirror, I only see the appearance. I can only paint my image. I'll still be able to do justice to you, though—with your husband's permission, of course."

"But what will happen now?" Elise asked. "To me, I mean? Now that my grandfather is dead."

It wasn't over, I realized. Not unless Tommaso and Lorenzo had gone down in the conflict too. She still had a family, linked to her by blood; they would still have a legal right to claim her; they didn't even need to be above the law, in the sense that her father had been.

"I think you'll get to choose," I said. "Tommaso and Lorenzo don't have the reputation of being good or reasonable people, but they're not as bad as they paint themselves, let alone as others paint them. They won't do you any harm."

"That's good," she said. "It's good to be able to choose." She didn't sound entirely convinced, although it was the truth. She had never really thought before about having a choice in major matters, but had simply gone with the course of events, as children do, only exercising choice in trivial things, exerting her will just for practice. For now on, it would be different. From now on, she would have to decide what it was she wanted, not just from moment to moment and day to day, but with a whole future life in view.

"Shall we stop at our house or go on to yours?" Charles asked, as Jean-Jacques turned on to the promontory.

"We'll go on to Axel's," said Hecate. "Finished or not, his triptych will make a backcloth for our performance. It won't be the same as the marine trumpets, but the middle panel will help to put the language of sighs in context. As long as there's a good fire in the studio—now that it's getting dark, it's turning positively Arctic."

Luzon had, in fact, kept the fire stoked up in anticipation of my returning with guests. She had even prepared a meal, which was more necessary that anyone had anticipated. Danger of death stimulates the appetite, presumably because of all the extra energy released by the rush of adrenalin.

So we ate first, and calmed down, until we were in an appropriate state of readiness to hear Hecate and Elise perform, after which we arranged the triptych as a backdrop, even though two of the panels were still incomplete.

As the child picked up her bow, though, I couldn't help feeling a twinge of apprehension, thinking that the instrument was still essentially diabolical, and the language of sighs still the language of screams.

XVII. The Truth About Orpheus

This time, when the bow stroked the strings, there was no scream. There was nothing discordant in the sounds that Elise drew from the accursed instrument, which seemed, at last for a while, to switch into angelic mode. The music that poured forth was unadulterated sweetness: genuine charm, although not without a hint of compulsion. It was pure temptation, but so pure, so unadulterated, that it was utterly confident in its own irresistibility.

When that girl wants to be seductive, I thought, *in the full sense of the term, no one is going to be able to resist her.*

But for the moment, at least, she didn't want to be seductive, in any erotic fashion. The purity of the music persisted; it drew the mind in but without the mind knowing exactly where it was going. I had no doubt that Elise was improvising, and not only because there was no music-stand in front of her carrying a score. The piece was not being invented momentarily, however; she had played it before, exploring it with Hecate's company, under Hecate's guidance. It was a collaborative endeavor. I knew that even before Hecate's voice joined in with the strange melody—if "joined in" is the correct term for a combination that was more opposition than fusion, more contest than collaboration.

Hecate was not singing, or even reciting in the manner that I had heard her recite her work a hundred times before. When she had said that she was working with the language of sighs, she meant it literally. What was doing with her voice was wordless, but it was not

232

meaningless. I understood immediately what she had borrowed from the eerie voices that had echoed so strangely in Vashti's séance, unconsciously channeled— or so it seemed—by Mariette. Those really had been the voices of the dead, in some sense, even if they had originated and Mariette's throat and Mariette's unconscious, but this was Hecate's voice, and Hecate's voice alone, consciously produced, as a work of art. It was remarkable, to be sure, but it was a performance, pure and simple. It was a poem of sorts, improvised but rehearsed, practiced and supported by Elise's music, to which it was a kind of counterpoint.

What, I wondered, would the marine trumpets have contributed?

It wasn't hard to guess. The marine trumpets would have been the other shades, in the crowd scene represented in the middle panel of the triptych. They would have been the background hum of the Underworld, incidentally subdued by the music that Orpheus was addressing primarily to one of them, or perhaps to two: to Eurydice and to Hades, the latter envisaged symbolically as the death that had her in his grip.

As the piece was being played now, though, there was just the music of the substitute lyre, and the presence of Eurydice, as a shade, in the clutches of death. The remainder of the Underworld and its population had been reduced to mere paint and charcoal, not even finished.

The sweetness of Elise's music was devoid of any erotic quality because it was charming death, not love; it was pure, because it was dealing with life itself, not the pleasure of life, it was weaving existence, not ecstasy.

And Eurydice' reaction—her reaction, not her reply—was a litany of sighs.

And suddenly, it became obvious to me what I had been missing, even though it was right under my nose, even though it had been voiced in my presence, and I had voiced almost all of it myself, under Dellacrusca's needling, and had almost made it manifest at the tip of my brush: the truth about Orpheus.

It was something that I was composing, of course, with the aid of Elise's chords and Hecate's sight; it was a work of art, not a literal representation of something that had actually happened three or ten thousand years ago, but that didn't make it any less true: quite the contrary, in fact.

Orpheus had been romanticized. The idea of him charming the beasts, causing even the trees and the rocks to follow him, had been envisaged by his admirers as a pleasant and amicable endeavor, a benevolent induction of affection, a bountiful taming of savagery, a generous contribution of life to dull inertia. It had been seen as marvelous, enviable magic, which made Orpheus a beautiful and virtuous person.

But in reality, as I had suggested to Dellacrusca, it was all about control, command, and possession. It was all about making the animals, and the birds, and the trees, and the very rocks do what he ordered them to do. Orpheus wasn't a beautiful and virtuous person at all. Orpheus was a Dellacrusca.

Even his supposedly heroic deeds, such as shielding the Argonauts from the Sirens, were a matter of asserting control, a matter of competition and mastery, of demonstrating the power of compulsion.

And as for the excursion to the Underworld: what heights of arrogance! He had gone to subject death itself to his command, to compel Hades, the personification of death, to release Eurydice, to give her back to him.

Why?

Because he loved her, of course. But what kind of love was it? Not my kind, for sure. Dellacrusca's kind. Possessive love; love that demanded obedience, compliance; love that insisted on molding its object to a rigid framework of desire planned in advance, and love that would brook no contradiction.

I understood, as Hecate had, the texture and the nature of Eurydice's lament. I understood how the nymph had really died: that she had not been bitten by a snake at all, but struck dead by a single angry, screaming chord of Orpheus' lyre, when she told him that she no longer wanted to be subject to him, that she wanted to be free. Passion had overwhelmed him, and anger had caused his fingers to lash out, at an instrument that had the power to charms and compel every animal in creation... and, in consequence, the power to kill.

Doubtless he had regretted it at a moment after he had done it, because he really did love her. Doubtless, he had been heartbroken as well as wrathful—but what had his reaction being to the realization that he had killed the thing he loved most in all the world, in a fit of stupid petulance? To mourn? No—not for an instant. To strike back, to demand from the death itself the reversal of his own recklessness. He had plunged into the Underworld, ready to do whatever it took to undo his fatal reflex, to charm death itself, and to command Hades to let one victim go: just one; the one that Orpheus considered to be his property. No benevolence there—a kind of love, yes, but no benevolence.

And he had succeeded. He had charmed the shades. He had charmed Hades himself; he had learned and mastered the language of sighs and had turned it to his own purpose. And Hades had been forced to let his precious prisoner go, *even though she did not want to go.*

But Hades—Death—had provided Eurydice with an escape clause. He had disguised his permission just sufficiently to tempt Orpheus to a violation, to allow Eurydice to pause, and not to cross the threshold of life into the particular kind of slavery that Orpheus had in store for her.

Did she regret that? Of course. She had loved Orpheus in her fashion, which was as real, in its own way, as his, and perhaps more real, depending on one's definition of love. Would she have regretted surrendering to his domination and control even more? Yes. That was not the kind of life she wanted. It was not the kind of life she could accept. Her lament, from beyond the grave, was a lament for the impossibility of her predicament, for the terrible situation in which Orpheus' obsessive, all-consuming, all-devouring and all-demanding love had placed her, because rather than in spite of the fact that she loved him too.

It was easy enough, too, to fill in the end of the story. Orpheus had succeeded in bending Hades to his will. He had exercised his power of command over a god— and that was not something that could be done with impunity. Orpheus had thought himself invulnerable, that there was nothing beyond his control, but he had been wrong. He could not control or command madness. He could not command or control maenads. Even Hades could not really command maenads—but he could inspire them. He could aim them, like a weapon, and let them loose.

So Orpheus had died, and his severed head had floated down the river, still singing—or possibly screaming—with the image of Eurydice, his personal Nemesis, still in his eyes.

It made sense. At least, it made sense to me. It made sense as a work of art, and was therefore true, in my eyes.

And when Hecate ceased sighing, and Elise laid down her bow, I sighed myself, not merely with satisfaction but with relief, at having been delivered from the monster named enigma, the insidious poisonous reptile that had been undermining my endeavor.

I was being selfish—but all artists are egomaniacs, even those capable of a truer love than the perverted phantom that some consider "true" because it cannot tolerate dissent.

I did not have time to collect the impressions of the other members of the audience, because the harsh sound of the doorbell cut through the soft silence left by Hecate and Elise, jerking all of us out of a light esthetic trance.

Jean-Jacques answered the door, and ushered in Tommaso Dellacrusca.

"Are you all unhurt?" was his first question.

"Yes," I replied, on behalf of us all. "Not a scratch between us."

He sighed himself, with genuine relief. "That's good," he said. Vashti Savage is unhurt too, and Niklaus Hylne. We killed all eight of the Dionysians, but they got five of his, including Father and Mesmay, and wounded a dozen more. Lorenzo got a bad gash on his arm and lost a lot of blood. They got the parchment too—they couldn't take it away, but they tore it to pieces. Fortunately, we still have two fine copies, made by a consummate artist. They have one, taken from the Convent, but perhaps, on due reflection, that's not entirely a bad thing. It might help ease the competition and prevent escalation. Luckily, Fion Commonal was on hand in the ballroom, and he organized the help for the wounded. He stitched Lorenzo's cut himself, but Lory had to lie down. Commonal says that no one else is likely to die, but even so, covering up what happened is going to be the Devil's own job."

"Covering it up?" I said, incredulously. "There must have been forty people there, at least, maybe fifty. Your father, Mesmay and three others are dead. How on earth can you cover it up?"

"Apart from the insiders, two unattached members of the Council and the people in this room," Tommaso said, in a perfectly level tone, "there was only the medium and Hylne. We can keep the Council members and Hylne quiet easily enough—and none of you, including Vashti Savage, have any interest in spreading the story, or contradicting whatever fictions we concoct to account for the five deaths—which will, you understand, all take place elsewhere, in our version."

"What about the Sisters of Shalimar?" I said, skeptically. "You don't think they'll be concerned about the violation of their convent?"

"Of course they will," Tommaso replied, "but being concerned and kicking up a fuss are two different things—and they didn't see what happened at Mesmay's house. Aethne went round there as soon as the last Dionysian was dead. The nuns were distressed, understandably, but not hurt. Even the Dionysians have limits they won't cross. The Mother Superior will know everything soon enough—Aethne will need her counsel and support more than ever before, now—but she has no reason to challenge publicly whatever version of events we come up with. It's vitally important, you understand, that the affairs of the cult remain secret, especially in an instance like this."

I wasn't at all sure that I did understand, and I certainly didn't sympathize. "You can't possibly control the servants," I told him. "This is Mnemosyne. The story will be all round the island in a matter of days."

"The story is all around the island right now that the Devil has extended his cloak over the island, blotting out the sun, that the reek of brimstone is everywhere, and that plague and pestilence are about to descend. Do you think, in the midst of all that, that anyone on the mainland, let alone the Capital, is going to take seriously a story about a gang of maenads disguised as nuns attacking the audience at a concert? Even the people telling the story won't believe it—and even those who saw it happen will begin to doubt it, when it's juxtaposed with the version to which all the surviving members of the Island Council, the widowed Marquise of Mesmay and a dozen other respected citizens will swear. You, of all people, Master Rathenius, should know that the truth is just the work of art that everyone agrees to believe."

I spread my arms wide in a gesture of helplessness.

Tommaso walked past me then, and went to confront his niece.

"We haven't even introduced," he said. "I'm your Uncle Tommaso. I wish that I had time to spare to get to know you, but things are very complicated at the moment, and my brother and I have to get back to the Capital as soon as possible. We inherit the money and the property automatically, but all the rest—all the positions he held in the government and the society—are going to be the object of fierce competitions, which Lory and I can't possibly win. We'll have to work hard to clarify our new situation. But I don't want you to think that we've forgotten you, or that we don't care about you. You're family. At the very least, we'll see you next summer, and every summer, when we come to spend time here. In the past, we've only come to lark around, and it will be different from now on, but we'll still make time for a little amusement. And when things have settled down, there'll be opportunities for you to visit us in the Capital, if you wish."

He turned to Charles Parenot and Mariette who were standing together. "On behalf of my brother and myself," he said, "I'd like to thank you both for taking care of our niece for all these years, while she was lost, and we'd like to beg you, if you don't mind, to look after her for a little longer—with our help, although that will have to be at a distance for a while. We never met our sister, or her husband, so we're happy to regard you as her mother and father, and as honorary members of the family. If there's anything you need, don't hesitate to ask."

He shook Charles Parenot's hand, and actually kissed Mariette's wrist before turning once again, this time to Myrica Mavor.

"I have bad news for you, I fear, Madame Mavor," he said. "The commissions you discussed with my father are null and void—and to be perfectly frank, Lorenzo and I thought the fees that he offered were too high. We are, however, willing to discuss the possibility of commissioning a portrait of Elise to be painted by her father, for the family gallery, at a reasonable price. We'd rather, however, that it's a formal portrait, without the musical instrument. As for the Marquis of Mesmay's triptych, we'll guarantee that you and Master Rathenius receive the remainder of the fee, whether the Marquise wants to take delivery of it or not."

"What about the other portrait?" Myrica ventured, ever the agent. "Now that Mariette is an honorary member of your family, she wouldn't be out of place somewhere in your principal residence."

Tommaso weighed that up for a moment. "We can discuss that too," he said. "But not here and not now. Come to see us in the Capital, after the funeral. I have to say, though, that we have no interest in a mythological painting of Persephone. We'd prefer a picture of Madame Parenot as herself—and it seems to me that Master Rathenius would be better able to paint that than her husband, who might not be able to see her with such a clinical eye."

He turned back to Elise. "May I give you a farewell kiss, until we meet again, my Niece?" he asked, politely.

"Of course, Uncle," she replied, and offered her forehead, which he kissed very decorously.

He nodded to Hecate, and said: "I'm sorry that your performance was spoiled, Mademoiselle Rain. I hope to see it this summer, during the season."

She nodded in reply.

"Show me out, Master Rathenius," he said, a note of command creeping into his voice for the first time.

At the front door, as he peered into the icy darkness, he said. "Are we even now, Master Rathenius?"

"Better than even," I assured hm. "I'm in your debt."

"How am I doing, as Lord Dellacrusca?"

"A magnificent performance," I said. "I knew that you had it in you, but it's a privilege to see it. You say that you have two copies of the enigmatic text?"

"We've recovered Hylne's," he said. "We didn't think that the Dionysians even knew what had happened, but we assumed that if they did, they'd go for that one, so we set an ambush there. We really couldn't imagine that they'd go for the Convent instead, let alone... the rest. They're only bits of paper, when all said and done. Nobody is ever going to be able to read them, are they?"

"Probably not," I said, "Except..."

"Except that we don't know how the maenads produced that incredible scream. Dionysian craziness. Bizarre."

I couldn't tell whether he believed what he was saying, or whether it was just the story that he and his fellows were making up, or their own consumption and satisfaction.

He took a step into the night, but then paused and looked back. "I'm glad she's here and not living on the Mount," he said, softly. "She'll be a lot safer, especially with you nearby to keep an eye on her. You will do that, won't you, Master Rathenius?"

"Certainly," I said. "But I won't be able to resist her any more than anyone else. One day, she might be Empress, even without your father to mold her."

He shook his head, but not because he was denying my assertion of possibility. He found the whole thing incredible. Perhaps it was.

"They must have really wanted to get back at your father, and make a point," I observed. "Did he, perchance, order the poisoning of the late Monsieur de Toustain when Guillot first told him who he really was?"

Tommaso shook his head. "I really don't know," he said. "But I wouldn't put it past him."

Neither would I, but I saw no need to say so.

Tommaso raised his hand in a polite salute. "I have a great deal to do, Master Rathenius. You might not see me again for some time."

"Don't worry," I said, "I won't forget you."

I closed the door, glad to shut out the cold and the dark—but Charles Parenot and Mariette were right behind me, with their honorary daughter.

"We'd better go home now," said the painter. "Elise needs to go to bed. Thank you—for everything."

"I didn't do anything," I said, realizing with a slight pang of regret that it was true. I had worked no magic and employed no cunning. Hecate had done something, and Tommaso Dellacrusca had done a great deal, as had Elise, but I had been a mere bystander. Even my heroic gesture in saving Hecate had probably been superfluous.

"I look forward to sitting for you, Master Rathenius, if Madame Mavor can strike a deal with the new Lords Dellacrusca," said Mariette, with deliberate politeness, as she left.

"As do I," I assured her, and kissed her hand, as Tommaso Dellacrusca had done. I only patted Elise on the head, though; she wasn't my niece.

When I had shaken Charles Parenot's hand and the door had closed again, it occurred to me that even though the twins were identical, and had been born mere minutes apart, only one of the "new Lords Dellacrusca" could, in law, inherit the title and the entailed fraction of the estate. I hoped that the twins would settle things between them amicably, without either one feeling compelled to murder the other. Perhaps, as I was the only person in the world that could tell them apart, they could take turns.

"You must both stay the night," I told Hecate and Myrica, when I leaned my head round the studio door. "It's far too cold and dark for Jean-Jacques to take the carriage out again. I'll tell Luzon to make up beds for you and light fires in the rooms to take the chill off them."

Having done that, I went back to the studio.

They were both standing in front of the unfinished triptych.

"You might not even have to finish it now, if Aethne de Mesmay doesn't want it," Hecate observed.

"I shall finish it," I said. "It was a challenge, which I accepted—and thanks to you, I now have the narrative complete in my mind. It won't be obvious to people looking at it, but you and I will know the true story. Thank you for that."

"It was just a reflex action," she said, with a half-smile.

"I was thanking the reflex action," I said, responding to the cue.

"You two really ought to get married," said Myrica Mavor, who hadn't understood the narrative at all.

"Why spoil a beautiful friendship?" said Hecate. "In fact, Axel, I'm rather tired, after that performance. Sighing is surprisingly energy-consuming, by comparison with merely talking. Do you mind if I go to bed right away"

"Not in the least," I assured her, and kissed her on the cheek.

When she had gone, I looked at Myrica. "Well," I said, "things seem to have worked out well for you, at least. The new Lords Dellacrusca might strike a slightly harder bargain than their father, but they could well be good clients for the next twenty or thirty years, and they'll always know that you and I know one of their darkest family secrets."

She studied me for a few seconds, and then said: "You can drop the act, Axel. I know you did it. The others have no suspicion, but I was here. I saw you, remember."

244

"I haven't the faintest idea what you're talking about," I told her. "What am I supposed to have done?"

"You killed Dellacrusca."

The enormity of the accusation took my breath away. When I got it back, I said: "How am I supposed to have done that?"

"By means of sorcery," she said. "I watched you. You even said, in so many words, if I remember correctly: 'If I could stop it by sorcery, I would.'"

"If *I* remember correctly," I said, "I finished the sentence by saying that I couldn't."

"But you were actually doing it as you spoke, weren't you. You were painting Dellacrusca as a severed head, torn off by maenads."

"And you really believe that with a mere twitch of a paintbrush, I conjured eight maenads out of thin air, and immobilized the Sisters of Shalimar while my phantoms stole their habits and marine trumpets? Come on, Myrica—that took planning, and incredible daring, but it wasn't sorcery. Insanity, yes, but not sorcery. And I can assure you that I have never killed anyone in my entire life, and hopefully never will—not even a Dellacrusca. If I really had been able to stop him by sorcery, do you think I'd have gone about it in such a barbaric fashion, and killed four innocent people along with him, not to mention the maenads? That takes insult way beyond mere wordplay, Myrica. It's a monstrous suggestion, as well as an insane one."

"Oh, I don't say that you did it consciously," she said. "You're an artist. Your whole *modus operandi* is to give your unconscious free creative rein to manufacture narratives. But you must have realized, as it was happening, that your wish was coming true, albeit without your careful conscious scruples and inhibitions."

"You think I'm a sorcerer without even knowing it?

"Yes—just like the little girl. Perhaps Hecate too, in her way. Perhaps we all are, without knowing it—but sometimes, it becomes manifest, as it has three or four times in the last few days. Sometimes, these things just *burst* under pressure, like volcanoes. You can deny it if you like, but I saw what you did. I know."

"You saw me applying paint to a picture. It's what I do. There's nothing else to know, and there's nothing supernatural about it. If I have vision, and insight, it's purely natural."

"I see things differently. But you needn't worry. I'm your agent. My lips are sealed. No one will ever know what you did tonight—in fact, no one but a favored few will ever know what happened tonight, if the surviving members of the Cult of Orpheus have their way. For the world at large, it will be as if it never happened at all, so far as history is concerned. I wonder how many other things they've erased from history, over the centuries?"

Probably lots, I thought. *After all, if my interpretation of the myth is correct, their entire heroic history is a lie.*

And I sighed, deeply and meaningfully.